anne wheeler

A HOUSE OF NEBULAS

illustrated by
lara calleja

For everyone who still believes in fairy tales.

Once upon a time . . .

CHAPTER ONE

If anyone had told her back on Cereth that she'd one day be landing at the imperial palace in a shuttle for an official dinner with the emperor, Ryllis would have laughed at them. Yet here she was, climbing the steps to the formal garden in the center of the complex, wearing the most ridiculous costume she'd ever owned and clinging to the arm of His Imperial Majesty's youngest son.

Her husband.

It seemed like a dream sometimes, even though it'd been almost sixteen lunar rotations since their hasty and unplanned wedding in a clinic room. But the marble beneath her wasn't a dream, and the heavy scent of evening hydrangea and hyacinth in the night air wasn't a dream, and the filmy gown she wore wasn't a dream, and Kresten's presence beside her certainly was not.

Careful not to trip in her heels, she shot him a surreptitious glance. He was grinning at someone unseen at the top of the stairs—his height allowed him to see where she couldn't—and it was impossible to hide her own smile at the sight of his happiness. She hadn't thought she'd be able to smile when he'd first brought the black dinner jacket from storage. For reasons she could never have explained, the black fabric with gold embroidery on the collar and sleeves initially reminded her too much of his Fleet uniform, but now she wanted to run her hands all over it—and him.

I know you're staring at me, darling star. So inappropriate. Whatever will the rest of the guests think?

She missed a step when Kresten's voice broke into her mind, even though the reprimand was nothing but flirtatious teasing.

I'm not— She could feel herself flush, and *that*, everyone else would notice. *I'm not staring. Not everything is about you, Kresten.*

I suppose not. A telepathic chuckle echoed. *But you are. I can feel your eyes on me. But I can't blame you when I've been staring at you ever since you put on that dress. A pity I have to wait so long to take it off.*

How she wanted to roll her eyes—or smack his arm—but there were too many guests, too many sentries. She took a deep breath instead, cloaking her amusement in the exertion of climbing the stairs. The dress helped, too. The lightest blue and the most well-fitted piece of clothing she'd ever worn, the silk was dwarfed by the tulle overlay, studded with the traditional Vilarian pattern of stars and flowers. Seed pearls studded the center of each, and she had no doubt the candles made the dress itself glow.

Somehow, I think you'll survive. You always do.

Perhaps. With difficulty. Kresten squeezed her hand as they arrived at the top of the stairs.

"Are you ready?" he asked out loud.

She squeezed his in return and shook her head. In truth, she didn't know what to expect, no matter how much he and the palace staff had tried to prepare her. To have to make small talk with a crowd of Vilarians, for people to bow and curtsey to her—it was unthinkable. Kresten was still by her side, though, and with him there, she could survive anything. Had already survived. What was a formal garden party compared to being brought to Vilaria against her will? To almost losing her life? To meeting his father for the first time?

He brushed a brief, proper kiss on her cheek, then they were standing in the garden, people all about them. *Garden* was such a misleading name for the space, so large she couldn't see the other side. Lights hung from the mahogany trees that covered the entrance, making the gold on his jacket sparkle. Probably her hair, too, dark as it was. The trees were in full bloom this season, and it was difficult to smell anything besides their perfume. She tried not to gawk at the sprays of branches that hung above, dripping with gossamer filaments that effervesced and glimmered overhead. Candles sat on every available ledge, stone, and empty branch alike; she wanted to dance through them, the extravagance too enchanted to hate. Nature felt like this all the time, and now she was seeing it through her eyes as well.

In a place where magic was all but forbidden, it was . . . *magical.*

"Didn't I say you'd enjoy it?"

Ryllis tried to catch her breath again, though it was from the sheer beauty this time. Kresten's eyes were almost as wide as hers, and she had to remind herself that this wasn't something he was all that familiar with either. For the most part, he'd left his family a long time ago, had gone off with the Fleet to make use of his telepathic skills.

"It looks like magic," she said. "I can scarcely believe what I'm seeing."

"Told you so. Let's go look."

A servant headed them off as they made their way through the crowd. He bowed, then gestured through the small grove toward an ethereal white tent, also glowing with miniature lights. "His Imperial Majesty is already seated for dinner and has been asking for you both, Your Highnesses," he said. "If you'll follow me, please."

"He starts quickly, doesn't he?" Kresten asked. The servant frowned, and Kresten nodded his assent. "Yes. Of course. Lead on."

Best to get it over with now, he added to her. *Father is desperate to see you again, and I'm hungry, anyway.*

Kresten's love of food made her laugh out loud, and the rest of her anxiety fell away as she did. It was still odd to her that the Vilarian emperor was the one familiar thing in this nightmare of an evening, but it was a relief to be summoned by him so early—the summons meant she could put off small talk with strangers for a time. He'd even sent her a personal message earlier, lamenting that he hadn't seen his son much lately, and how he hoped this night would be a chance to get to know her better as well. She'd bitten her lip hard enough to draw blood, then made Kresten compose the reply.

I'm not afraid of seeing him.

Really? That's why I had to write our acceptance, isn't it? It's all right to be nervous.

Really. I'm nervous, yes, but I'm fine.

It was a lie, but she was becoming better by the second, which meant the palace staff hadn't quite suffocated the trees with the décor and that she could still feel their power. She closed her eyes for the briefest instant, letting their peace wash over her. It worked, as it always did, and she thanked the Light for allowing the party to happen in a garden.

I don't believe you're fine. You're just about to break my fingers.

"I'm sorry," she gasped out loud, relaxing a little of the pressure.

"Ah, there we go." Kresten breathed easier in her mind. "I'll need those to hold my fork."

The servant led them across a smaller path, then into the tent that was surrounded by the most discreet palace sentries Ryllis had ever seen. It was only her Cerethian background that allowed her to notice at all. As she'd told Kresten a long time ago, noticing when there was a representative of the Vilarian Star Realm around could mean the difference between life and death on their conquered planets. Everyone had become paranoid since they'd become part of the Realm.

Kresten dropped her hand. *Remember—*

Yes, yes, she replied. *Pretend I'm thrilled to be here and that I don't notice how they're all looking at me.*

I love you.

Love you, too.

The emperor was already seated at the head of the table, chatting with a noble Ryllis didn't recognize. He looked up at her and Kresten's entrance, then motioned toward them.

"You made it," he said. "I was beginning to wonder."

Her heart thumped against her chest as she knelt next to Kresten. The gesture had long since ceased to bother her—in private, at least, and there had been many private audiences with his father since their marriage—but tonight was different. All these eyes on her. She could feel them on her back, knew what they were thinking about her, even if Kresten's was the only mind she could read.

Cerethian trash.

Slave.

Whore.

What in the Realm was he thinking, marrying someone like her? Couldn't he have found someone here on Vilaria?

Maybe there's something wrong with him. He went off with the Fleet of his own free will, you know.

Before a single tear could fall, Kresten rose, and she followed a split second behind, resisting the temptation to touch her eyes. She hadn't been imagining it—the low conversation in the tent had gone silent for a heartbeat, and she wasn't foolish enough to think it was out of respect for a minor prince. The emperor held out his hand for both of them, though, and as she kissed his knuckles, the banter returned. Allowing her to do such a thing was an intentional move, she knew, and one of the few reasons she'd been brave enough to attend tonight.

You will respect me, he was saying to the others present. *Which means you will also respect my son and his wife.*

Or else.

Their emperor's approval of their marriage should have been enough, but as she sat next to Kresten on a hard, wooden chair and clutched her hands in her lap, she knew it never would be. The gossip and mocking would continue as long as she was on his arm, even though both he and his father made it clear that treating her as a scandal would not be tolerated.

A servant poured wine from over her shoulder, and Ryllis barely refrained from jumping at the sudden intrusion into her space. That was another oddity of her new life—while she'd expected Kresten's ability to speak directly into her mind to be disturbing and intruding, it always felt like an intimate and welcome caress instead. No, it was the constant presence of guards, servants, and slaves that grated on her nerves, for so many reasons, mainly because that subservient role had been hers for a short time after arriving on Vilaria.

That bothered Kresten, too, and that meant, thankfully, these uncomfortable social and political events only happened at the palace. Only Lina worked in the mountain lodge as his house-keeper, and the flat in Arvika was empty except for the two of them—Kresten had rapidly learned to enjoy her Cerethian cooking. The solitude and peace were a balm for both of them.

"I have an announcement for you all," the emperor said as Ryllis wound her fingers together in her lap. "And I wish I'd given my son more time to be prepared for the news, but the details were just worked out a few hours ago."

Ryllis's head swiveled toward Kresten, and he shook his in return, the smallest hint of a frown appearing.

I have no idea.

Her gut tightened. He rarely—never, that she could remember—spoke telepathically in front of his father, which meant he was concerned.

"As you all know, the situation on Cereth has proven most unstable over the past solar cycle. Since the attempted assassination I was subjected to a few solar cycles ago, it seems the separatist movement has grown, and grown violent. Attacks on our building, thefts of our military stores, propaganda like you can only imagine. This new philosophy is a curse, and it's spreading fast. We must do something, and we must do something soon. And I can think of no one more qualified to mitigate these issues, no one more capable of acting as an advisor to our troops and regional governors there than my son."

Beside her, Kresten stiffened. She wanted to touch him, wanted to console him, but she sat there properly, as a princess of the Star Realm of Vilaria should, extricated from reality, while her past and present collided.

"Therefore, I'm pleased to announce that His Imperial Highness, Captain Westermark, has been recalled to the Fleet, effective immediately, and will leave for Cereth in two solar rotations to take the position of military attaché there." The emperor's gaze fell to Kresten. "I am certain he'll prove to be a credit to his empire."

Like it had been pulled from the heavens on a string, reality smashed back into her like an asteroid. She'd thought the not-so-discreet stares of the nobles at the table had been bad enough, but this—this was the worst thing ever. They were supposed to return to Arvika tomorrow, to the quiet flat, to her container gardens and herb garden in the kitchen, to Kresten's leather-working hobby that was, he'd told her, the first enjoyment he'd experienced in a dozen solar cycles. It was all planned. His Majesty just *couldn't*—

But he had.

A deep ache began in her chest and she reached out a shaking hand toward her wine. The drink wouldn't solve anything, but at least it could numb the pain taking over her mind. It would give her hands something to do. Because she could already hear the stranger on her other side snickering under his breath, and slapping him was out of the question.

The tent grew dark around her, and with it, the pain grew more intense. And it was only when she knocked the glass to the table and the wine spread like blood on the white linens that she realized the distress she was feeling was Kresten's mental anguish.

The throne room was unusually hushed and shadowy. The emperor preferred to hold audiences with the lights on, the better for his subjects to see exactly who was giving them orders. It had never made sense to Kresten that anyone could forget who controlled their very lives, but then, not everything had to make sense where His Majesty was concerned. And the current darkness? Perhaps the palace servants had borrowed some lights for the garden across the way.

That inappropriate witticism stuck in his head, Kresten stood, hands clasped behind his back, while his father paced in front of him. He'd stripped off his dinner jacket—didn't even know where it was anymore—but he didn't care where he'd left it, nor that he'd never appeared before his father in anything so casual as the dress shirt that remained.

"This is not punishment," his father said, stopping in front of him. "Not in the least."

His mouth was too dry to speak. He tried anyway, wishing desperately it would be proper for him to move toward the pitcher of water on a side table.

"I resigned, sire. You know that. I want nothing to do with the Fleet, and I want nothing to do with Cereth."

"Your personal desires come second to the needs of the Star Realm, and your resignation can be rescinded." His father planted himself, finally, on the ornate throne against the far wall. "Your temporary freedom was always a farce, anyway. You serve the Fleet at the pleasure of the emperor—at *my* pleasure—since it appears you've forgotten. This news cannot have come as a surprise to you."

The way his father had ceased pacing was probably a warning, but Kresten didn't care. "Father—Your Majesty—please. If you're ordering me to rejoin the Fleet, I can handle that. I'll do it with no argument." That wasn't true, but the lie would go unknown for now. Once he'd escaped one part of the plan, he could escape the other half. "It's just . . . Send me anywhere but Cereth. It's— it's unethical. I'm biased. I cannot possibly discharge these duties you've assigned to me in an impartial way. You know that."

"That's quite the argument." His father's eyebrows rose in amusement. "I have to admit, I wasn't expecting it. No matter. I need someone I can trust, and I know you'll do your duty to the best of your ability."

Kresten sucked in a breath at the challenge. "You mean you know I'll cave to your orders, Father."

"I know my son's loyalty used to be impeccable. Tell me I wasn't mistaken."

Kresten's blood chilled, even though the evening outside was still warm. There was no way out, not when his father was making veiled threats about his loyalty.

Except perhaps . . .

"And what of Ryllis?" he demanded. "I can't leave her here alone. You saw how they looked at her as soon as she sat down. They hate her. I will not subject her to whatever treatment they might come up with without me here to defend her."

"Oh, please." The emperor waved his hand. "Ryllis doesn't need you to defend her. That girl is strong enough to handle whatever those idiots throw at her—but she can go with you, if you wish. The Fleet allows it of high-ranking officers, as you know, and if that's what it takes for you to accept this without further argument, I see no reason the same agreement can't be worked out for you. As much as I think you'd sometimes love to forget your imperial obligations, there will be social occasions outside of your Fleet work, and that will make a good argument for her accompanying you."

Had his father lost his mind?

"You're suggesting I take her to Cereth with me?" he repeated.

"Again—if that's what it takes for you to do this with a minimum of quarreling."

Kresten reached out mentally, but he couldn't feel Ryllis anywhere nearby, which meant she'd either fled home to the flat or had closed her mind completely to him. Maybe both.

Probably both.

"She'll never agree to that."

"Then she'll do just fine here on Vilaria. If it comes to it, you can send her back to the mountain, if she'll go, then she can avoid all the unpleasantness of Carilles. I won't hear any further excuses about this, Kresten. Three solar cycles. It's a long time away from home. You'd best begin gathering up whatever uniforms you have left and packing."

"Father—"

"I said that's enough!"

Kresten pressed his lips shut. There was questioning, and then there was patent stupidity in front of the ruler of the Star Realm.

"If it makes you feel any better, I'll say this once. I need you. There's no one else I can send. Not from the family, at least." The emperor rattled down a list of names. "None are Fleet, and none can be pushed through the required training in any kind of expeditious manner. None have the training and skills and connections that you do. None are appropriate for the position of military attaché."

Kresten looked down. "I will do this. For the glory of the Star Realm. But, Father—once it's over—I want it to be over. I will continue to serve you and the empire for the next three solar cycles, but after that, I can do this no longer."

"I decide that. Not you."

He nodded and stepped forward to kiss his father's hand. Deciding the conversation had ended was a risk, but he needed to flee. He needed to see Ryllis. And as he straightened and met the emperor's eyes, he knew he'd lost—and yet, he'd won.

You decide less than you think, Father.

CHAPTER TWO

Kresten had mentioned, once upon a time, that most people became used to the horrible lurching and pressure of the Fleet jumpships that traversed the network of wormholes infiltrating this part of the galaxy. It made sense. The Star Realm couldn't have conquered as many systems as they had unless their troops could survive this kind of thing multiple times—and then voluntarily agree to do it again. Even conscripted troops were useless if they were unable to walk once they reached their destination.

Still, Ryllis couldn't understand how that could be. As the ship accelerated to prepare for another jump, her body felt like it had melded with her seat, and the harness threatened to cut her in half. She tried to look at Kresten, but the acceleration had made her body so heavy that moving was out of the question. Asking for reassurance was impossible when her entire being had to focus on taking another breath.

Just one more jump and this would all be over.

Just one more a wormhole and they would arrive in orbit around Cereth, the sole planet revolving around its sun, and where she'd spent most of her life.

Before she'd been arrested.

Before she'd been sent to Vilaria as a slave.

Before she'd married Kresten.

She shouldn't be back here, not even close, and as her body became light again—the last jump was the shortest—the reality of the situation hit her. Kresten didn't know how long they'd really be on Cereth, and he didn't even know what he was supposed to be doing. He'd said it could be three solar cycles as a military attaché to the imperial governor of Cereth, and that was bad enough. But all he knew—all she knew—was that he was to report to one Colonel Berglund when they landed in Epuas, and that this Colonel Berglund would give him his official orders. Three solar cycles might have turned into five on their way here. There was no way to know what the emperor had planned for him.

And her? Kresten had been even more vague about what she was to do during her time on Cereth. She didn't need to work. Probably wasn't allowed to, both in her new position as a prince's wife and for security reasons. There might be a garden for her to play in, but she wasn't counting on that—and even if there was, how could she openly use her power on a planet where her gift had always been forbidden? The very idea of doing so when so many others could not sent waves of nausea rushing through her stomach. No, the only thing she was counting on was at least three solar cycles of boredom and depression.

And her family? Her heart flipped when she thought about them—they were landing in Therus, her father's district, after all. Her sister, estranged for so long anyway, would hate her for being here once she learned of Ryllis's fate. Rose—Primrose—had always vociferously opposed the Star Realm's presence on Cereth, steadfastly ignoring how dangerous her protestations were for herself and her family. That outspokenness was why their father had insisted Rose leave solar cycles ago. Her awful stepmother, Zaella, and her useless stepsisters Bry and Greta—

well, there wasn't any point in thinking about them. And her father . . .

"There will be a garden," Kresten broke in as the jumpship slowed even further in preparation for entering the atmosphere, "even if I have to dig up half the planet to make one for you. And you and I both know you don't have to use your gift. Your skills are amazing enough on their own, but if you can't help it—or if you simply want to—no one will question you. You're safe."

"You're eavesdropping again." She tried to smile, but her immediate future was too anxiety-inducing to mean it. "What happens when we land?"

He waved at their plain brown one-piece garments, typical civilian jumpship attire. "We change, naturally."

Ryllis grimaced. It was impossible to keep the ships cool enough as they traveled through space, and most passengers sweated so much the ugly brown things were a necessity. Kresten was not one of those passengers, though, and she hadn't been able to decide if his current lack of uniform was for her own benefit or his. A fresh one, adorned with his new rank, sat in a bag under his feet, though. He wouldn't leave the jumpship without wearing it, just like she had to make the same immediate royal impression to whoever was waiting for them on the surface.

"And then?" He was being deliberately obtuse, not that she blamed him. Or—the thought occurred to her as she pushed a timid foot at her own bag containing a change of clothing— perhaps he truly didn't know. How frightening of his father to have sent him to Cereth for . . . what?

"There won't be anything official—I made sure for you. It'll just be some quick introductions, enough to be polite, and then you'll head to the villa while I meet with Berglund."

Lovely. Her first hours on her home planet would be spent alone, or followed around by servants who weren't supposed to be there, which would be even worse. Vilarians despised her just for her place of birth and former status in the Realm—what would her own people think of her?

Well, that was easy enough to answer.

Traitor.

Collaborator.

Vilarian whore.

"Hey." Kresten turned her face toward him with a gentle hand, and she squeezed her eyes closed, shaking her head in a vain attempt to stop his comfort. "I know this is difficult, but we're going to make it, right? Things have been worse, and we've made it through those times, too. This is nothing."

"Kresten—they hate me. All of them." The inside of the jump-ship felt like it was boiling, and it wasn't the appearance of blue sky outside and the increasing atmosphere that had done it. She swatted a bead of sweat from her forehead and wondered how she was supposed to appear fresh and imperial once they hit the ground. "Your people think I'm beneath them, and mine think I'm a—"

"No." His expression grew hard, yet she knew it wasn't directed at her. "Do not think that word ever again, darling star. Strike it from your vocabulary. You are my much-loved wife and a welcome member of the imperial family, and you have done nothing wrong. Not in going to Vilaria, not by marrying me, not even kneeling for my father."

Her heart fluttered. She'd closed off her mind to him, so he hadn't heard the things she'd thought, but he knew her well enough to know, anyway. He knew her fears, her insecurities, her doubts—but more than that, he knew they weren't unfounded. It was the reason there were supposed to be no Cerethian servants waiting for them in the villa in the hills outside Epuas, but there would be security, both Fleet and local police. They'd all taken oaths to serve the Realm, to protect its emperor and his family, but would the Cerethian security personnel follow through?

It was a silly question. Naturally, they would, if not out of respect, out of fear for their own lives. Suddenly, as the ship shook and the alarm for the landing sequence began, she felt even more sullied. Would her own people think she now condoned everything the Star Realm did? Would they resent her? Would her and Kresten's lives be in danger because of who the people thought she was?

"I know I haven't done anything wrong," she replied. It was what Kresten wanted to hear, so she would agree with him, even if it wasn't the truth. She'd married a member of the imperial family, and in the eyes of every Cerethian, she'd committed an unforgivable sin.

"But we're going to talk about this tonight, all right? For now, we need to get ready."

He sighed, unlatched his harness, and reached for his bag. Heat swept over her anew as he pulled out his uniform and stripped off his clothes. Any other time, she would have had her hands on his bare chest, but this—now all she could do was watch with wide and stoic eyes as he transformed into the stranger she hadn't seen in an eternity. It was still Kresten's lovely face and his sad attempt at a familiar smile, but yes, in the blue jacket and silver-edged pants of a Fleet officer, he was a stranger again. The same as he'd looked when they first met, only this time she knew what the gold star over his captain insignia meant.

That subtle marking that she hadn't recognized when they'd met meant he wasn't just Fleet. No, he was Shadow Force as well, the elite group of Fleet telepaths who searched out treason and interrogated prisoners and handled . . . she didn't know the rest, but she knew enough to know that she didn't want to think of it. There was a reason Kresten had left that life. Well, that and the blackouts that happened after each interrogation. He was tired of them, and how could she blame him for that?

He sat back down next to her and finished buttoning his shirt before reaching for her hand. "No smile for me?"

Ryllis bared her teeth. It might amuse him more than she intended, but it kept her focus off the uniform.

"Well, that'll do, I suppose," he said with a laugh. "Your turn."

His love was enough to keep her from panicking as she replaced her jumpsuit with the dress and shoes she'd picked out back on Vilaria, so many light-years away. The dress was cream silk with a navy medallion pattern common in the region where they were landing, and the heels on the shoes were higher than practical. Both were expensive, clearly the fashion in Carilles, the capital of Vilaria itself, and both would look out of place on Cereth. But she and Kresten had debated her wardrobe over and over, and while there was enough Cerethian attire packed away in the bowels of the ship to last for quite a while, she needed to arrive as a Vilarian princess.

There must be no mistaking where you stand on Vilaria, Kresten had said. *Later, once we figure out how people are going to react to you, you can dress as you'd like.*

He was right, but as she ran her hands over the silk and smiled shyly at him, she couldn't help but feel like a doll, adorned and decorated and fake. Her hair was limp and slightly damp from the trip, but that didn't make her feel any more human. Kresten's eyes lit up, though, an expression she hadn't seen since they'd left Vilaria, and she couldn't resist. She spun around dramatically in response, ignoring how the movement made her sick on the steadily descending ship.

"If I didn't know better," she said, "I'd say you like what you're seeing."

Kresten bounded to his feet and grabbed her around the waist. "Come on, Ryllis. We have five minutes until we hit the ground, and you do this to me?"

You did the same to me, was the automatic reply on the tip of her tongue—but she glanced down before she could toy back, down at the blue fabric of her nightmares and that horrid galaxy on his chest pocket. Kresten must have caught her change in emotion almost instantly, because he led her back to her seat and strapped her in. She clutched at his arm, and he pulled her closer, steadying her.

Ignore the uniform.

She didn't know why he'd switched to telepathic speech, but she replied in kind. *Easy for you to say. They've never done awful things to you.* Too late, she remembered that wasn't true at all. *I'm sorry. You know what I mean.*

Kresten chuckled inside her head. *I know. But this will get better. It'll have to, right? It certainly can't get any worse.*

The alarm grew louder, and Ryllis twisted to her opposite side as the trees became larger, giving way to a landing pad. A small contingent dressed in blue stood there, though she couldn't count the exact number at their angle.

"They're waiting for us," she said, knowing he couldn't see from where he sat. "An entire group."

"Good."

He sounded tense now, even flinched as the ship hit the ground so gently Ryllis wouldn't have noticed except for the automated message above the control panel. A valve popped somewhere, releasing the rest of the pressure on the ship and flooding her ears with discomfort. It was no wonder they frowned upon interstellar travel on Cereth. Beyond the conquering and death and war, it caused more mundane issues—ear pain, exhaustion, and the inability to shower en route.

On second thought, maybe an empty villa with a large, empty bathtub wouldn't be the worst thing in the Realm.

Kresten kissed her cheek one more time and sighed. "That's it, then. Ready?"

Ryllis shook her head.

"Me neither," he replied.

He stood anyway and pressed the button to open the door like he'd done it a million times before. Ryllis supposed he had. She was jealous of his ability to turn on his duty like a switch—something she'd never been forced to do, had never even considered having to do. But Kresten had been raised that way, and she had been raised . . . to what?

To hate the man she'd vowed to spend the rest of her life with.

Fresh air flooded the jumpship, and she stood on shaky legs. Kresten motioned her toward the door. Three men stood on the landing pad, and they drew back when Kresten escorted her down the stairs. She released his arm at the appropriate time, and with a salute, he turned toward a man with silver braid down his sleeve.

The man saluted back, then held out a hand to her, smiling. "Aron Berglund. Welcome back to Cereth, Your Highness. We're thrilled to have you here."

Her heart skipped a beat. Was this man mocking her? Right in front of Kresten? There was a warmth in his eyes, though, and she could almost feel his thoughtfulness. It was too hard to conceal her confusion as she nodded back. This was a Fleet officer offering kindness?

"I'm happy to be here." Anyone could tell it was a lie, but she would play the game, just like Kresten did. "Thank you for the warm welcome."

"I'm afraid I need to borrow Captain Westermark for a while," he replied, waving toward one of the younger officers in a Shadow Force uniform. "But I'll have him back to you as quickly as possible. I'm certain you'd like to rest after the trip, anyway. Lieutenant Wikström will see you to the villa and make sure you have everything you need."

Ryllis wanted to argue. But when she looked up at Kresten, his face was solemn, and a rush of fear coursed through her. He was as anxious as she was, and they needed to get through the remainder of the day. Then they could collapse together. She nodded at the young officer who appeared at her side and followed him into the waiting car.

Berglund's office wasn't very far from the landing pad at the local Fleet base, and it hadn't taken long for the usual Vilarian hospitality to be initiated. Being served by a higher-ranking officer was unheard in the Star Realm under most circumstances, but the rule was relaxed after an interstellar voyage, something Kresten had always found amusing. He downed his second cup of strong coffee and chuckled as the colonel placed one more on the table beside him.

"I've had plenty, sir. Any more, and I'll begin shaking."

Berglund shrugged and swiped the cup, taking a sip himself. "That's right. You're used to jumping, and I have to say, I'm fairly jealous of that skill. In that case, I suppose we can get right to it."

Setting the coffee on his desk, he swiveled toward a locked case behind him and withdrew an unmarked datapad. Kresten folded his hands in a desperate attempt to appear uneager. The man wasn't tormenting him with his apparent leisureliness, but it certainly felt like it. Maybe things were just like this on Cereth now.

"Here you go," Berglund said, handing over the pad. He pressed his index finger to the reader, and Kresten did as well. "And before you ask, no, I don't know what's inside either."

"Something important, sir," Kresten murmured, as the screen came to life. It had to be especially important if they hadn't sent the information to him on Vilaria. Then again, Berglund wasn't Shadow Force, and he'd likely never met the emperor in person. Colonel or not, he didn't have a need to know until Kresten arrived and decided he did.

"Indeed." Berglund leaned back and folded his arms.

Kresten ignored him and scanned the message, his dread growing. It had to be a sick joke. The expected military attaché position was listed first, naturally, but these orders had specifics.

Specifics the emperor hadn't mentioned that evening in the throne room.

"You knew nothing about this, sir?"

Berglund shook his head. "What is it?"

Kresten's mouth went dry, and suddenly, turning down that third cup of coffee seemed a mistake. He stood and reached for it, not caring that Berglund had already taken a drink, then paced.

"You know Governor Camden, yes?" he asked.

"Naturally. He might be Cerethian, but he's served the Star Realm faithfully for a long time." Berglund's brows drew together. "What's this about?"

"They want me to investigate him, arrest him, interrogate him, then bring him to Vilaria for trial. This—I don't understand. This can't be right."

Berglund frowned. "Maybe they know something I don't. I don't have to tell you that he's not the only Cerethian who's ever fallen under suspicion, and far be it from me to question the High Command. Why can't it be right?"

He couldn't throw up in front of a senior officer, but he was so close. Kresten glanced around the office for something other than coffee, but there was nothing. He swallowed the sourness in his chest and put a fist over his mouth.

"Because he—he's my wife's father."

CHAPTER THREE

No servants greeted her and Wikström when he opened her door inside the gated drive. His security detail remained outside as she explored the villa, though he trailed behind the entire time, and a little of the pressure eased from her chest at Kresten's promise. The house wasn't Kresten's secluded lodge in the Kebnekaise mountains by any stretch of the imagination, but that was the only thing Ryllis could find to grumble about. Like all Vilarian seasonal homes for Therus, it had a large front patio, a central courtyard with a gushing fountain, and picture windows in every room.

Even with her father's relative wealth, almost unknown on Cereth, they could have never afforded such luxury. The open living area gleamed white, another contrast to Kresten's warm home, but the live greenery that hung over the fireplace and the intricate mosaic tiles decorating the walls warmed it to an acceptable level and kept her from hugging her arms around herself. Luxurious fabrics covered each piece of furniture, and Ryllis found herself both missing the rustic painted chests at home and wanting to run her fingers all over the aqua velvet.

And the kitchen. With no servants, she'd be doing most of the cooking herself, and she couldn't imagine a more beautiful place to do it. One long island ran down the center, topped by a single piece of polished wood, the swirls and eddies reminiscent of the ocean whose waves could just scarcely be heard in the distance. She hadn't realized she'd missed the homey aesthetic. The cabinetry was a soft cerulean, the same color as the ocean over the distant hills. Kresten must have agreed to pay a fortune for them to stay here.

"Who owns this place?" she asked Wikström. The idea of someone having been made to move out by imperial degree was unsettling.

"The crown. The kitchen is stocked," he went on without missing a beat, pointing to a datapad by the deep freeze. "But if you need anything else, you can add it here."

She opened a few drawers, studied the fish and vegetables. All familiar, and for the first time, she was grateful they'd landed in Therus. Cuisine on Cereth had never been cosmopolitan, and the Vilarians didn't understand that. Their own planet had grown into one large city as far as culture went, and the regional and district differences of some of their own colonies baffled them. Explaining to him that she scarcely recognized some of the ingredients from her own planet would have been a lost cause.

"I can't shop for myself?" she asked.

Wikström looked at her as though she'd just asked if she could chop off her arm in front of him. "Of course not, Your Highness. It wouldn't be safe."

Ryllis stared at him from across the kitchen. Surely, he knew her story. But he was watching her with wide-eyed innocence tempered with puzzlement, so perhaps he truly didn't understand that this was her home. She waved him off, exhausted from holding herself together in the proximity of his uniform, then filled a glass with ice water and padded to the center of the house. It was strange to have security outside here, on her own planet, even though she'd grown used to the palace sentries during her infrequent visits to the imperial residence. Emperor's son or not, security didn't follow Kresten around the galaxy while he did his Fleet work, so they must be here for her.

Or—an even worse thought occurred to her as she chose a chair next to the fountain—perhaps there had been threats. The slightest shimmer of a force field sparkled above her, so there was nothing to fear from that direction, and as she stared up the olive trees in the courtyard, she almost convinced herself there was nothing to fear, period.

The sunlight certainly helped. It warmed her face like the thin mountain air at Kresten's lodge never really had, and there was a tang on the wind, courtesy of the Ishas Sea just a kilometer away. She reclined, letting the magic of the trees and sea breeze wash away the remaining horror of the jumps. It should be more difficult returning, but the pressure and disorientation were already fading away, urged on by the power of nature. Her mouth watered, even though she hadn't tasted olives with any frequency until Vilaria. Olives on Cereth were for the wealthy.

With that, the peace of the courtyard flashed away. She was on *Cereth*. Her home. Her father, sister, stepmother, and stepsisters were here, on this planet. Her mother was buried here, and she'd spent lunar cycle upon lunar cycle imprisoned here before being sent to Vilaria as a slave.

A commotion inside the house caught her attention, and she pulled her shoes back on before heading to the foyer. Wikström stood there, his hand pressed against the comm in his ear and his other hand gripping the arm of a young girl, not more than twelve. One of his men had her by the collar of her dirty dress, and the girl screeched again as she kicked at him.

"Is there a problem?" Ryllis asked.

Wikström jerked upright, as if her shoes hadn't alerted everyone within five kilometers of her presence.

"No, Your Highness," he replied. "Simply handling a trespassing issue."

For whatever reason, he didn't shove the girl to the floor in front of her like she'd expected, and for that, Ryllis was grateful. That someone had entered the villa without security noticing? That, she wasn't as grateful for.

"We were told the villa was too secure for trespassing."

"She knocked, ma'am."

"Knocked? Then it wasn't trespassing, was it?" Ryllis focused on the girl, whose thin face tracked with tears. "Who are you? Why are you here?"

"I didn't know anyone was here. It was supposed to be empty except for the caretaker. He—"

"He what?" Ryllis asked.

"He gives us food. From the vegetable garden out back. I didn't know he was gone! I meant no harm."

"You steal it, you mean," Wikström growled.

"No!" Panic crept over the child's expression, an all too

familiar sight for Ryllis. "There's plenty, too much for one person, and he said he couldn't stand throwing it out. I stole nothing from the crown, I swear!"

Ryllis waved off the man holding her collar and studied the girl. She was scrawny, but no thinner than half the girls she'd known at that age. But the dirty clothes and fright she exuded left no doubt something was terribly wrong.

"What's your name?"

The girl paled. "Alessia."

"Alessia." The name sounded foreign on her tongue, Cerethian or not. Had she become that Vilarian in that short a time? "Well, if you're hungry, we'll go look at the garden later and see what we can do. But first, I want you to take me to your house."

Wikström had protested—of course—but she ignored him and followed Alessia down the curving roadway. It was hot, but the sea breeze went a long way toward mitigating the warmth. More difficult were her shoes, completely useless on the cobblestone street. It was hard to keep up with the girl, who skipped barefoot over the rough stones like she'd been doing it her whole life.

Alessia led them through and into what could be graciously called an alley, surrounded on both sides by ancient buildings at least five stories high. They had been beautiful once, with arches, windows, and intricate iron bars along the balcony and stairwells, but time—and perhaps the Vilarian occupation—had not been kind to them, for the stone was crumbling in places, the iron rusted. The high stone blocked the wind, and broiling fish and human waste replaced the scent of the ocean as they walked.

Behind her, Wikström coughed. Ryllis didn't know why—it wasn't as though Vilarian smoked cod smelled much better.

"Here it is."

Alessia waved them through an open doorway, into a single

dim room. The walls were the same brick that made up the outside of the row house, though they were smeared with grime and cooking grease. The cause of that grease was an open fireplace at the far end, to the left of one more door, where sunlight shone through.

Ryllis headed there, already claustrophobic in the small house.

"How many live here?" she asked, sticking her head out the back door. A poor attempt at a garden surrounded by a low stone wall greeted her, along with a mangey goat that bleated sadly at her as she walked outside. Her udder was wrinkled and deflated, and when Ryllis ruffled her head, the goat butted against her hand.

"Seven," Alessia replied, as Ryllis knelt down to give the goat more scratches. "My parents and brothers and sisters. But they're working, and—and looking for food."

Begging, she meant.

"But please," she went on, "leave Lavinia alone. She—she bites when she's hungry."

"I don't think she'll bite me," Ryllis murmured.

Indeed, the doe was nuzzling and licking her hand, leaving streaks of saliva. Ryllis wanted nothing more than to wash her hands, but if the animal was benefiting from her gifts, so much the better. A quick glance told her Lavinia's eyes were already clearing up, so Ryllis perched on the wall and let her bask in whatever magic she could take.

"She must like you." Alessia's eyes were wide. "She hasn't liked anyone in a long time."

"She must." The girl didn't need to know about her powers. "How long have you lived like this?"

Alessia looked at the ground. "A long time."

Ryllis wanted to sigh at the shriveled vegetable plants that clung to a set of sticks in the shade of the house. She could heal them, but to what end? Would they survive after she left Cereth?

After she left Cereth.

Blinking back tears, she pushed Lavinia away and inspected the plants. They were alive, though if Alessia's family expected to get any food from them, they were going to be sorely disappointed. In the house's shadow, they were starved for sunlight. It was understandable—placing them in full sun meant hauling more water outside, but it was the only way.

"Here's what we're going to do," she said, pretending Wikström wasn't leaning against the doorway frowning at her. "You're going to help me move everything"—she spun around, then pointed— "right here, and then we're going to sit here and talk a while." Plopping herself down in the middle of the relocated garden would give the vegetables enough of a head start, and Lavinia wouldn't be unhappy at her new source of energy either.

"Ma'am." Wikström finally spoke. "This isn't necessary. They'll get on, like they did before you arrived. Perhaps you could send someone to help, if His Highness approves."

"His Highness does not own me."

A poor choice of words, for Wikström shifted on to his left foot. Wonderful—he knew everything. Knew that at one time, Kresten had.

"Of course not, ma'am," he said.

Ryllis dug up the first of the tomato plants with her hands. "But I'm here now, so why not help?"

He shrugged and joined her and Alessia, carting the uprooted plants to her choice of location next to the wall. With three hands and a spoon from what passed for the kitchen, it was quick work, and Ryllis wiped her palm over her damp brow as she sat on the stone once more.

"Then that's that," she said. The plants were already looking better, and by the way Wikström was glancing between them and her, he'd figured out it wasn't just from moving them. "They'll do much better now. Haul some water back for them, Alessia, and while you do, I'll put a basket together for you from the villa."

The little girl looked like she wanted to kiss her, but she backed away, nodding, then disappeared into the house.

"What are you doing home, you lazy urchin?"

Memories of Zaella bursting into her mind, Ryllis jumped to her feet at the shout and somehow beat Wikström back inside. Alessia was pressed against the wall. The older woman shouting at her drew back as Ryllis entered, then sneered.

"And who is this?"

Ryllis held out her hand. "Ryllis—" Not Camden. Realm's sake, she couldn't be known here as Camden, the pathetic excuse for a governor. But not Westermark, either. Not yet. "Just Ryllis."

"Where did you come from?"

The villa up the hill, seemed to be the wrong answer. "Zralt District," she said. "I'm visiting. I met Alessia, and I thought maybe I could help."

"We don't need help. We—"

The woman went pale, and Ryllis turned to see Wikström at her side. *Fabulous.*

"You," she shouted at Alessia again, then grabbed her by the throat and shook her. "What in the Realm is the Fleet doing here? You should know better!"

"He was helping us, Mama," Alessia cried.

Wikström, to his credit, pulled her off the girl and shoved her away. She muttered something unflattering in an almost-extinct Cerethian dialect, then spat at Alessia's feet.

"Vilarians don't help us. We've taught you better than that." She turned to Wikström, still pale. "What has she done, Lieutenant?"

He looked at Ryllis, like she was the one responsible for the entire mess—which, she supposed, she might be.

"Nothing. She's done nothing. And you'd do well to keep your hands off her," he warned. Then, to Ryllis, "We really should go, madam."

She nodded at him, then Alessia. "I'll bring that basket by later."

"No." Alessia's mother pointed at the door. "You won't. Now get out."

Kresten dropped his jacket on the living room sofa and called Ryllis's name. She didn't answer, and it was five minutes of searching before he found her in the bathroom, half-hidden in the soaker tub under a pile of bubbles. She smiled at him when he entered, then laid her head back against the tub and closed her eyes.

"Rough day?" he asked, sitting on the edge next to her. "And here I thought you'd be enjoying that courtyard."

"Don't stall. What happened with Berglund?"

He sighed. "Ryllis, it's . . ."

"Classified, yes, I know. But give me some sort of hint."

He traced a finger along her jawline, leaving a streak of bubbles in his wake. "I don't know what to say. Anything I tell you will upset you, and—"

"I know."

"It's the resistance movement. Someone rather high up they'd like me to investigate. That's all you need to know."

Her eyes became puffy as she pushed herself out of the tub, and he couldn't blame her for that. As furious as he was about being forced back into the Fleet, it was a thousand times worse for her to be back on Cereth as the wife of an occupier.

No. That wasn't right. Vilarians married locals all the time. That wasn't so unusual. But being married to a prince, someone who had actively persecuted her people in the past? He couldn't imagine her emotions, even though she let him feel some of them.

Ryllis grabbed a towel, and he wound it around her, then kissed her ear.

"I suppose I don't want to know more," she said. "Please don't tell me."

It was an easy enough request, especially when she dropped the towel and walked into the closet to study what had already been unpacked.

You're staring.

Can you blame me? he asked.

A wave of sadness rushed over him, followed by a telepathic smile.

No, she said. *But let me fix something to eat first.*

Fair enough.

He massaged her shoulders as she reached for a clean dress, only backing away as she moved to pull it over her head. The desire to tell her his secret was painful, and he used the separation as a chance to push his emotions down, hide them the best he could. Stress was acceptable for a Fleet officer and prince. Even fear. The sickness he felt, that certain sense of betrayal deep in his soul—that was not.

Ryllis turned back to him and gave him a peck on the cheek. "I hope you're not expecting this to taste like anything at home. I doubt you'll recognize half the things in the kitchen."

Kresten grinned. "I'm sure we can come up with something decent."

A laugh echoed in his head. She pulled him to the kitchen by his hand and stood him in front of the cooler while she pulled a few things out.

"Olives," she said, handing him a small bowl.

He curled his nose at the astringent yet fruity scent. "They smell awful."

"Because they're not cured with the lye your people are so fond of." Ryllis popped one in her mouth. "Delicious."

He couldn't help rolling his eyes. "What else is there?"

She stared inside for a moment. "Chicken?"

"Perfect. You know I never turn down chicken."

Ryllis laughed out loud. Kresten chopped the olives—breathing through his mouth, of course—while she tried to figure out the oven. Chicken roasted with olive oil and topped with olives wasn't high on his list of favorite foods, but as she triumphantly brought out their meal, he had to admit it looked delicious. Maybe it was just that both of them had been frightened by the other things in the cooler.

He sat next to her at the island, wanting to touch her, wanting to tell her—but he kept his gaze focused on the chicken instead. In the corner of his vision, Ryllis took a few bites, then set her fork down.

"I've been thinking."

"About?"

Her bare toes scratched along the wood floor. "Am I supposed to visit?"

She didn't need to be specific. "I hadn't thought about it. Do you want to see him? We can certainly arrange it."

His chest grew tight. A visit could be useful to him professionally.

"How do you think he'd react if I did? Do you think he knows what happened to me?"

"I don't know how he'd react . . . but I'm certain he knows what happened."

Ryllis's father was the governor of Therus, after all, puppet leader or not. Someone in the Fleet would have told him about her imprisonment, enslavement, and eventual marriage.

"He hasn't tried to contact me."

Kresten ran his fingers along hers. "Do you want to see him?"

Ryllis's eyes met his, dark and worried.

I don't know.

Her emotions fell into him in a chaotic heap, fighting each other for dominance. There was anger and fear, which he'd expected, but the yearning was the worst. She'd never stopped missing and loving him, the man responsible for her arrest and exile, and she was afraid—no, *terrified*—that he still wanted her gone.

Kresten wrapped his arms around her and pulled her close, letting her sob against his shirt. He had less than charitable thoughts about his own father, but what was he supposed to have done? Likely it hadn't even been his idea—this was the Fleet's doing, no doubt about it. All he had to do was prove Camden's connections to the resistance, then he and Ryllis could go home. And home was Vilaria, not the forsaken planet where everyone hated him, and she couldn't walk ten steps without memories assaulting her.

Yes. That was how this would go.

"I have an idea." His heart skipped a beat. *Such a thin line . . .* "I don't need to start this new project for a few days. Tomorrow, Governor Camden will receive a summons."

CHAPTER FOUR

In the end, Camden hadn't fought the summons, and Kresten almost wished he had.

Instead, the governor arrived on the front steps of the villa two solar rotations later, just on time. Kresten should have been out on the front steps waiting, but Camden was the least of his worries right now.

Ryllis was his main concern.

She stood motionless in the kitchen, her hands palm down on the polished piece of wood. It was only to keep them from shaking, he knew—for even though she'd closed off her mind, he could read her expression a little better these days. Laziness was a drawback of being a married telepathic, and something he'd always wondered about. It was too easy to rely on telepathic speech instead of those facial tells and body motions that begat intimacy.

"What am I supposed to say to him?" she asked quietly. "How am I supposed to act?"

"However you want to act." He leaned his back against the counter next to her and folded his arms. "What do you want to say?"

She blew out a breath, half laughing, though it didn't sound amused. "Oh, so many things, most of which would probably get me slapped or thrown in prison."

He gripped the edge of the counter so hard he was afraid he'd break it. "That will not happen ever again. And I despise the man with every fiber of my being for frightening you enough to believe it might."

"It happened before." Her eyes were wide and dark as she stared at him, almost confused. "I was able to pretend for so long that he had nothing to do with the accusations and my arrest, but he was behind it all, wasn't he? He turned me into the Fleet."

Shadow Force had told her as much during her telepathic interrogation back on Vilaria, the records said, but she'd never mentioned it since, and Kresten hadn't brought it up. What good would focusing on that kind of pain do? He'd read the transcript and almost punched a wall himself.

He gave her a tight smile, not even daring to reach out for her. "He was, darling star. I don't know why—whether he was protecting himself or simply wanted you out of the way for reasons I won't even guess at."

Since his conversation with Berglund, he had guessed, of course, and even had his own private theories, but Ryllis didn't need to know about them. They were official Star Realm business anyway, weren't they?

Yes.

"I wish I knew why he did what he did." She edged toward him, and he wrapped his arm around her. "I suppose the reasons don't matter, but I can't convince myself of that. What if it's something I did wrong? What if I truly deserved it somehow?"

"You can't let yourself believe that." Kresten lay his head on top of hers. "You didn't deserve any of that. At all."

Ryllis was silent for a moment. "But it brought me to you."

"I wish it had been in a different manner." The wish was

foolish—he'd have never met Ryllis otherwise. "But I won't lie, I can't imagine life without you."

She shifted toward him, and he could feel her body relax against his. Somehow, he'd said the right thing. And now . . .

You don't have to do this. The switch was abrupt, but some things needed to be said under his breath. *I'll send him away if you need me to. Just say the word.*

I think seeing him is something I need to get over with, and quickly. I can't have it hanging over me for another six lunar cycles. She squeezed him tighter, and his heart did that strange thing it usually did when she switched to telepathy. *I'm just so afraid. I think I know how it's going to go, but the smallest bit of me holds out so much hope, and I hate myself for it.*

We all have hope, he said, *about one thing or another.*

But even Rose wouldn't visit, and she never accused me of treason and terrorism and Realm knows what else. She said she had no desire to be in the same room with—well, I won't tell you what she called you. How can I believe any differently of him? He must hate both of us. Me for whatever I did and you for whoever you are.

We can debate this forever, but there's no way to know how he'll react until it actually happens. Which is now, as long as you give me the okay. Your sister— He sighed and brushed the hair back from her forehead. *She made a poor decision. That's not your fault. It's all on her.*

Not that the truth would make her feel any better. He'd ranted for a long time when Ryllis had told him the evening before about her sister's message, even threatened to arrest her so she had no choice *but* to talk to his wife. Ryllis had finally cracked a smile at that, even though he hadn't been joking at all.

I know it is. She kissed his cheek and pulled away. *You should go meet him. The governor does not like to be kept waiting.*

He wanted to chuckle at her choice of words but ran his fingers down her jaw instead. *You're going to be all right?*

Of course. I've been all right through worse than this, haven't I?

He didn't believe her, wanted to tell her there was physical pain and then there was emotional pain, but he gave her a kiss of his own and left her standing alone in the kitchen. There was an unfamiliar transport outside in the circle, and the man who emerged when the front open door opened looked exactly as he had in the pictures and reports Kresten had seen. He was dressed in a tailored suit with fur trim along the sleeves and wore the most ingratiating smile Kresten had ever seen.

No surprise there, from what little Ryllis had said of him. That also meant, probably, that the man had no idea who else was inside. Camden wouldn't be this smug if he knew he was about to be confronted by the daughter he'd sent to almost-certain slavery or death.

"Your Highness," Camden said, with a polite nod as he came up the stairs. "I was surprised—but thrilled—to hear you were on Cereth. I would have come sooner to welcome you had someone properly informed me of your arrival. But no matter. What's done is done. What can I do for the emperor?"

Sycophantic bastard.

Kresten swallowed the words he really wanted to say. "His Imperial Majesty has appointed me military attaché to the governor for the next three solar cycles. Fleet business isn't as glamorous as my other role, unfortunately, but I do what I can— for the good of the Star Realm, of course."

He didn't have to explain anything to Camden—his new, much less royal role should have been obvious from the lack of imperial sentries in the house—but he needed to make the stakes clear to the man. No, today, it was Fleet guards on either side of the doorway, and they followed him and Camden inside without a word.

Despite the politeness Ryllis had begged him for, after Kresten's brief interaction with the governor, he couldn't already help but think the man would look much better with a few black tattoos on his forearm. Ryllis would be devastated at the outcome, no matter how she thought she felt about him now, but it would put a quick end to things. Unfortunately, an immediate telepathic interrogation was not Shadow Force policy, so the circles would have to wait.

Kresten gestured Camden through and into the living area, and Ryllis's fear washed into him like an incoming tide.

Head up, he told her. It came out as an order, and he felt her flinch from the kitchen. *Sorry. Didn't mean it like that.*

"Fleet business?" Camden asked at last, settling into the armchair by the window, uninvited. Well, Kresten couldn't argue that kind of behavior in front of a lowly Fleet captain—he'd brought that on himself. "What kind of business?"

"Classified, I'm afraid." Kresten chose the sofa across from him. Plenty of room for Ryllis to join him when she chose. A united front. One Camden couldn't break. "And nothing very interesting, to tell the truth. I'm sure I'll have plenty of opportunity over the next few solar cycles to speak with you on a professional level, but this is more of a social visit—I'd be remiss to not invite the regional governor for some Vilarian hospitality, wouldn't I?"

"Hmm." Camden's eyes narrowed as he tapped on the side table next to him with an idle finger, likely waiting on a nonexistent slave to bring him a drink. "I suppose so," he said. "How are you finding Cereth so far?"

Ah, things were going perfectly now. Almost as if Camden was in on the surprise himself—which was a ridiculous idea. He had no clue, thought he was in charge of the conversation. It wasn't the first time someone had treated Kresten as though he was someone to be manipulated, and he'd long since ceased to be offended by it. Predictability was simple to handle.

"It's a lovely planet, especially here near the sea," Kresten said. It was hard to keep the grin from his face. "Though not much different from last time I was here, to be honest. I was hoping for snow, but it looks like I'll have to wait a little longer."

"You've visited before?"

"I was stationed in the prison in Vreir for a while. Not so long ago." In fact, sometimes it seemed like it had just been a lunar cycle or two. "It was—let's call it educational. This is, of course, a much more pleasant assignment," he said, as if to himself.

"Vreir?" Camden went pale at that, then recovered more quickly than Kresten had expected. "Well. I'm sorry that was your introduction to our fair planet. I hope we can show you this time that Cereth is more than criminals and traitors, Your Highness."

"Oh, I've no doubt it is." He tilted his head toward Camden in feigned curiosity. "You've been to Vreir? You seem familiar with it, but I wouldn't have thought you'd have traveled so far from Therus." Most in the Vilarian Star Realm weren't allowed to travel outside of their districts. Prisoners were an exception.

Camden paled again, and it was only Kresten's long experience in social interrogation that kept him from bursting into laughter.

"No," he said. "I've never been there. I've heard of it, of course. Everyone knows of the Star Realm prison there."

"I see." Kresten let his voice chill a bit, like any prince reminding his potentially wayward subject of his possible dark future. "Well, enough of that disagreeable discussion. Would you care for a drink, Governor?"

Her cue.

Kresten could feel Ryllis's anxiety increasing by the moment as the clicking of her shoes on the marble grew louder. Camden glanced out the window at the swaying olive trees outside, clearly unaware of her presence as she swept into the room, a drink in her hand.

If the man didn't recognize her immediately, Kresten wouldn't have been surprised. She hadn't yet opened up her trunk of Cerethian clothing, and the gauzy blue-green dress she wore, embroidered with gold constellations of his own system, was pure Vilarian royalty. She wore it well, even uncomfortable with the frills as she still sometimes was, better than he could have ever imagined. She didn't need the gold and embellishments in order to be the loveliest thing in the room, of course, but sometimes her eyes lit up when a new dress appeared and that made the cost worth it.

Anything that made her eyes light up was worth it.

"Thank you, yes, Your Highness. I'd like a drink." Camden's stare pivoted from the olive trees toward Kresten again; it was no surprise he was ignoring the appearance of a servant. "You know, if you're here for so long, you might have the opportunity to—"

Before he could finish whatever inane suggestion he'd planned, his gaze drifted to Ryllis. His mouth dropped open, and he drew his arms toward himself, his eyes bulging.

A pleasant feeling began in Kresten's chest and worked its way up and down. So, the governor hadn't had any idea what had happened to her, after all. Yes, perhaps surprises were sometimes still amusing.

"Hello, Father." Ryllis's voice was composed as she set Camden's drink down next to him. She took her place on the sofa next to Kresten, crossed her legs more elegantly than he thought possible, then nodded in Camden's direction. "Your drink. Please enjoy."

I love you, Kresten broke in, too rashly. *I'd grab you and kiss you right now, but he might have a stroke if I did, and that would be hard to explain. Lots of paperwork, you know? And I do hate paperwork.*

A light telepathic touch brushed against his mind in return. Ryllis couldn't laugh, not in front of Camden, but he'd amused her despite everything.

"You—" Camden actually sputtered as he glanced between them, his eyebrows drawn together and his brow furrowed at the casual proximity of prince and servant. "You—what are you—"

Yes, this was better than he'd ever imagined.

"Governor Camden," Kresten said, with the eager joy of someone who, in utter obliviousness, thought absolutely nothing was wrong with the situation, "I'd like you to meet my wife, Her Imperial Highness Princess Amaryllis."

"Wife? Princess?" For almost a full minute, Camden stared at both of them, his mouth opening and closing like a suffocating fish netted in one of the high mountain lakes of the Kebnekaises. "I don't know what to say," he finally said. "I—I hadn't expected—"

"You could start with 'congratulations.'" Ryllis's eyes filled with tears as she spoke, and Kresten reached, stopping just short of grabbing her hand. She was doing fine on her own. She needed to do this on her own. "Or perhaps simply 'I'm sorry.'"

"Sorry?" Camden's stiffened in his chair as his cheeks grew red. "What in the Realm do I have to be sorry for, you traitorous witch?"

It was Ryllis who was stricken speechless that time, and a sudden burst of anguish overwhelmed Kresten's mind. He pushed himself off the couch and loomed over Camden, his rage building, too fixated to answer her back or calm her.

"That's enough," he said. "You will refer to my wife by her proper title, you will stand for her, and you will show her the respect she's entitled to."

"Respect." Camden scoffed, but he sprang to his feet. "Why should I respect her? Because you call her royalty? You can't honestly believe I'm going to bow down and kiss the feet of our invaders. There are expectations, and then there's reality—and I won't do it to my daughter."

Another flash of pain shot through Kresten then stopped like a door had slammed. Ryllis had cut him off.

"Yes. Because of that. I know you're smart enough to understand what's at risk here." His voice was too loud, but he couldn't stop himself. "But more than that, you ought to be happy to treat her with whatever deference you can dredge up from the depths of your dark soul because she's your daughter!"

"Not anymore. You all took that away from her—or have you already forgotten how poorly slaves are treated on Vilaria?"

Was the man obtuse? Kresten clenched his fists, lest they meet Camden's nose. Not that anyone would say a word to him about it. Berglund might, but it would never make it into his official file. Not after he told everyone the entire story.

"She ended up in that situation because you falsely accused her of treason," he snarled. "Your own flesh. You knew what would happen to her after you reported her, and you did it anyway. How could you? How could you do that to someone who loved and trusted you, despite how you've treated her for most of her life?"

He didn't need to feel Ryllis's anguish any longer to be destroyed inside—he could feel his own. He could see her standing in front of the Eradication Council, waiting to hear her fate, he could see her sitting on the edge of his tub in the mountain lodge, sobbing after he'd cut off all her hair, and he could see her laying on that gurney at Fleet headquarters in Arvika, condemned to death because of her gifts. All because of the man standing in front of him.

Camden crossed his arms and lifted his chin. "Well, it certainly seems she didn't do too poorly for herself in the end."

"You don't get it, do you?" Ryllis's presence appeared in the corner of his mind once more, but he ignored it. "You don't know what she went through. You don't know what happened, what I had to do for her to even begin to fix what you destroyed. I—"

He broke off.

I hurt her.

I humiliated her.

I made her cry.

I held her while she sobbed.

I told her she was still beautiful.

I let her know everything would be all right.

I almost watched her die, just to save my life, and there was nothing I could do to stop her.

Those things—they were all too intimate for Camden to hear. They belonged to him and Ryllis now. If Camden had apologized, perhaps, showed the tiniest scrap of guilt, then maybe . . . but he didn't deserve any glimpse into a life he'd written off.

"If you can't appreciate how wonderful and loyal your daughter is," Kresten said, suddenly exhausted, "then I don't know what to tell you."

Kresten, just tell him to leave. He's not worth the argument or the hurt. I should have known better, and now I just want to be alone. Well, not alone. With you.

He didn't want to tell the man to go. He wanted to slug the bastard with all that was left of his remaining strength. But he felt Ryllis's pleading deep in his soul, so he did nothing more than put his arm around her shoulder and walk her out to the courtyard.

He would deal with Camden later.

CHAPTER FIVE

he lounge chair was big enough for two, and Ryllis was grateful for that as she curled into Kresten's body. The sea breeze blew her hair haphazardly, and she closed her eyes as Kresten ran his fingers through it and tucked it behind her ears.

"I should have known it would go that way," she said, forcing the tears away. His touch helped with that, but it wasn't enough, not while the hurt was still so raw. "I don't know why I expected anything else. When I first arrived on Vilaria, when I was prepared to be a slave for the rest of my life, I accepted never seeing him again, and while I didn't want to accept it, it was still easy. So why is it so difficult now?" Kresten didn't answer, and she blew out a deep breath. "Perhaps he'll change his mind and come back."

That was a lie, and they both knew it.

"It's difficult because you have a heart." Kresten's tone was curt, but she knew it wasn't directed toward her. "And because you're human. We cling to hope, even when it makes little sense. We don't have any other choice."

"I'm sorry he was rude to you, too." A small part of her was still anxious Kresten would hold that against him. It was too hard to forget her husband's planet controlled her father's. And Kresten *had* joked about arresting Primrose . . . or had it truly been a joke? "I'd never expected him to treat you so poorly. Even he should know better than that."

He rolled toward her and wound his arms behind her head and neck, pulling her close. "Nothing your father can say to me will hurt my feelings. I'm used to this kind of thing, believe it or not."

"I know you are."

It was a simple statement, but it chilled her. What was she doing here on Cereth, being held in the arms of a man who belonged to the empire who'd oppressed her people for hundreds of solar cycles? How could he claim to love her and do what he did? But he'd resigned from the Fleet for her. He'd sacrificed for her. That had to mean something.

You're upset about something else.

She tried to shift away when his voice entered her head, but his warmth was too alluring.

I'm not. Just him.

Don't lie. He traced a finger along her jaw, and she shivered.

It's just—being here. All of this. I don't know how to explain it, and I'm scared to.

Then don't try. Can I?

She nodded, and his touch flitted through her mind like butterflies in an autumn garden. It was intimate, yes, which was uncomfortable even now, but so much easier than verbalizing her distress.

And faster. It was only a few moments before the feathers in her brain stilled and he kissed her forehead.

I love you.

Even with those thoughts? Even though I still hesitate when I kneel before your father?

You're not the only one who hesitates, believe me. His laugh echoed in her mind. *Would you believe I do sometimes? By the Realm, I almost told him off the night he announced this assignment. Anyway, I'd worry if you didn't have those doubts—they only show how loyal you are. I married you. I wanted all of you, even your history and your doubts. I still want all of you.* There was a pause. *And that Cerethian chicken you made the other night. Why would I settle for someone who could only cook fancy, royal Vilarian food?*

Ryllis punched him in the arm, and he chuckled and pulled her a bit more upright.

"Let's go for a walk," he said. "Away from the villa. What do you think?"

"Really?" If Kresten went with her, security wouldn't need to. She could already taste the freedom of a long walk with him— something they weren't able to do very often unless they were in the mountains. Even in Arvika, people stared when they were on the street, and she could never decide if they knew him as a prince or Shadow Force officer. Neither one was appealing. "No one will recognize you?"

"Here, on Cereth? I'm the ninth child of the emperor, might I remind you." He grinned, jumped to his feet, and held out his hand. "It would flatter me if they did."

Ryllis put hers in his, warmed by the feeling. He still cared for her. He still loved her. She clung to that feeling as they headed through the house and she tried to forget everything that'd happened earlier that afternoon. Kresten waved off Wikström and the security team as he led her outside, and she took a deep breath of the sea breeze blowing across the expansive front porch.

"I miss the mountains," Kresten said, as they made their way down the steps. "But at least this is beautiful, until we can make our way back home and hide for a few lunar cycles."

He was right. From here, the top of the hill overlooking the village, it was certainly lovely. The dirt and grime of the alleys that surrounded Alessia's house weren't visible from the distance, and the vista looked like a priceless painting. Olive trees blew in the breeze, and she reached up and ran her fingers through one's lower branches. The tall wall around the villa should have made her feel trapped, but the clematis vines were in bloom, turning the pale bricks of her luxurious prison into a work of art. How could one feel trapped by fuchsia petals?

The wooden door that would have clashed with the pink in any other part of the planet already stood open—Wikström must have been expecting a food delivery—and she practically skipped through it without waiting for Kresten to follow. There was simply too much to explore. They might have landed in her father's district, but his home was in the woods of north Therus, nowhere near the sea. They'd visited a few times, back before Zaella had appeared out of nowhere and charmed her father into marrying her. Just she and Rose and their father sitting on the beach, pointing at how the clouds made pictures in the sky and chasing the small ghost crabs that darted across the sand.

Ryllis's powers had been as unpredictable then as always, but she'd felt comfortable and safe on the beach. There were no plants to respond to her on the dunes, and when the crabs approached her, unsteady and oddly sideways, her father had only laughed. He hadn't figured it out.

Kresten latched the door behind him and appeared at her side as she picked her way down the cobblestone sidewalk. One rolling cart passed them by, pulled by a Cerethian cow with shaggy brown fur and horns the length of a person's legs. Shuttles and cars, of course, were only authorized for off-world Vilarians or by a permit from the Star Realm. Her father had one, but most of the district did not. It was just one more means of oppression and a way of limiting resistance movements, but Ryllis had never minded. Who wanted to pay for a shuttle when they could sit in an open carriage and feel the breeze?

The cart driver gave her a short wave, then looked away, as if he'd suddenly realized she wasn't someone he should associate with. A half second from waving back, Ryllis clenched her fist at her side, but Kresten took hold of it as she watched the cart roll on. She glanced at him. There was no way to hide her shame.

He hates me. He knows what I am, and he hates me.

He doesn't know you. Only what he thinks he knows, and he's wrong about that. If he knew you, the real you, he'd know you didn't deserve any of it.

She sighed and swung his hand as they walked. *You're right.*

I'm sorry. We're not going to solve this today. Let's just enjoy the sun, yes? Did she dare take him to Alessia's house? The goat and garden could probably use her power. *There's somewhere I want to show you.*

Then lead on.

And she did, into the village down the hill, through the dilapidated alley. She could feel Kresten's curiosity through their telepathic connection, but he said nothing about their surroundings, even when she stopped in front of Alessia's open doorway. Perhaps that was part of love. He trusted her. Cared for her. Believed she was always trying to do the right thing, even after he'd met her in a prison, of all places.

The room that doubled as a house was empty except for a figure huddled on the mattress in the corner. Blankets were piled on top, and she couldn't tell if it was Alessia or one of her siblings. Definitely a child, though, and though it felt uncharitable to admit it, even to herself, it was a relief to not see the mother.

"We should go," she said quietly to Kresten. "We should let her rest."

The figured stirred at her voice, the blanket moved, and Alessia stood, blinking away sleep. Her eyes widened immediately when they landed on Kresten and the imperial crest on his jacket, and she lowered herself to her knees, eyes cast downward.

"You don't—" Ryllis began.

Let her do it, Kresten broke in. *It seems to have eased her fear, strange as that sounds. I suppose any other way would leave her suspicious and frightened I was walking her into some sort of trap.*

He made a comment to Alessia, likely to rise, but Ryllis was too distracted to hear it. She'd hated Kresten at first. A few small pangs of sympathy for his position had floated into her mind when she'd first arrived on Vilaria, but her own hate had swiftly overtaken it. What must it be like to feel the fear people had for you? Compassion for both of them flowed over her as Alessia rose and tried to smile.

"Did you come to see the garden, Your Highness?" Her eyes lit up, like she'd suddenly forgotten who Kresten was and that she'd been afraid of him. "Please, you must come see."

Kresten furrowed his brow, but followed her and Alessia out into the back garden. When her eyes adjusted again, Ryllis couldn't help a gasp.

The small courtyard, so brown and yellow when Ryllis had first arrived, couldn't be called anything but verdant now. The leaves of the olives had burst out, the vegetable garden was fairly loaded with tomatoes and cucumbers, and even the seeds Alessia had planted in small pots on top of the wall sparkled with color. Lavinia stood by the edge of the low wall, munching on lettuce. She turned at the sounds and bleated at her intruders, then darted toward Ryllis.

"You've been doing some gardening, I assume?" Kresten's eyes sparkled as she tried to swat the goat away. "I'd wondered what you'd been up to. I suppose I shouldn't have."

Ryllis tried to close her mouth. "We only moved some plants into the sun and sat with them a while. It was nothing. Just a long afternoon. I can't believe—it all happened so quickly!"

So did my mother's meadow sweetvine, he reminded her. *I wonder what the difference is.*

She shook her head. *I have no idea.* Her gift had always been quite random and unpredictable. It was hardly any wonder her mother had banned her from the garden as a child. Everything in nature reacted to her presence, but sometimes she could actually see a flower grow, and sometimes another plant would take weeks to show any unnatural growth at all. She'd spent a dozen solar cycles trying to determine a pattern, but there was nothing. Age, size, season, there seemed to be no trend. She'd accepted that a long time ago, as frustrating as it was.

Alessia grabbed her by the hand and pulled her toward the

wall. "Look," she said in awe, pointing down the slope on the other side. The vines must have been there before, but they had to have been half dead for her not to notice. Now they were covered in large green leaves and the faintest hint of the beginning of fruit. "Grapes. They've never grown here. I don't understand."

Ryllis glanced at Kresten, and he put his hands on his hips, amused, though she felt his undercurrent of concern. Alessia would panic if she told her what had really happened, but there wasn't anything else to do.

"Well, the plants . . ." She drifted off and glanced around. Someone, probably Alessia, had even staked the new vines. "They like me."

Alessia frowned. "They like you?"

"They grow better when I'm around." How was she supposed to explain this? "All plants do. Animals, too. I couldn't leave Lavinia looking like she was, couldn't leave here without giving your family your source of milk back. So yes, while moving them into the sun helped, so did my presence. That's partly why I sat out here for so long that afternoon."

Alessia took a step back, toward the empty doorway at the rear of the house. "Presence? You did this? You have an innate power?" the girl whispered.

Ryllis nodded.

"I can't believe it." Alessia was pale now. "Does—does the prince have one?"

"No," Kresten cut in. "Just her."

Ryllis wanted to correct him for accuracy's sake, but Alessia didn't need to know about Kresten. Shadow Force was known and feared on Cereth, and Alessia would make the immediate connection, just like Ryllis had so long ago. She pressed her lips closed and nodded at Kresten's claim.

"But innate powers are illegal. Everyone knows they're illegal." Alessia sounded frantic. "And you used yours here, and now

—what if the Star Realm finds out what happened here? What if they think one of us did it? What will they do to us?"

"Nothing. I did it, and it's not forbidden for me." *Not any longer.* "And I'll tell anyone who asks."

"It's not an issue," Kresten added. "I'll make sure of that. Any issues with the Realm, any problems with the Fleet, they will be taken care of."

"But—" Tears sprang into Alessia's eyes. "My mother's already so angry you were here. If she finds out you did this, she'll—she'll beat me."

Kresten's anger washed over her, and she closed off her mind. Her own rage was too difficult to deal with, especially when the memories of how Zaella had treated her snuck in. "Then she doesn't need to find out who did it. Has she been suspicious?"

Alessia shook her head.

"Then we'll go." Ryllis motioned Kresten back through the single room. "And if she raises a finger toward you, come to the villa and let me know. Or one of the security people, if I'm not there. They'll have orders to take care of it. I'm sorry."

She stalked into the alley, Kresten's footsteps right behind.

"That's it?" he asked, furrowing his brow. "You're just going to let it go?"

"What else can I do?" she growled at him as they headed back down the alley. "Anything I try will only make things worse. And what was I supposed to do before? I couldn't live up there in that villa, knowing a bunch of children were living like they were. Not when Alessia first showed up and Wikström almost yanked her arm off, and not when I first visited and saw the conditions they were living in. I did a favor, and even those always end up backfiring in the end."

"Not always." He pulled her to a stop and pressed his lips to the side of her mouth. "You did a good thing," he whispered in her ears. "Judging by the state of that home, I can only imagine what the garden looked like when first visited. How can anyone deny you did the right thing?"

"The garden was bad." She untangled herself from his arms and looked around the alley where they stood. He'd probably never seen—or smelled—anything so rundown. Neither had she, to tell the truth. *It's all bad, Kresten. Just look at it.*

You blame me for this, he said. *And the Star Realm.*

It wasn't a question, and he spoke a prohibited truth, and yet she trusted him enough to let her questioning show.

I don't blame you. I don't even solely blame your father, not exactly, though I do more than I suppose is safe. I mostly blame—I don't know who or what. Blaming people and blaming a culture doesn't change the past, and it doesn't change what's happening now. Even if things change on Cereth and everywhere else, I won't live to see it, and that's so difficult to accept.

None of us live to see large changes like that. Kresten sighed out loud as they turned onto the main street. *But things will change. Remember? You and I are proof of that. It may take a hundred solar cycles, but things are changing.*

Alessia could still end up a slave. It only takes such a minor mistake —sometimes it takes nothing at all. She can be the most loyal Star Realm subject in the empire, and it won't matter if she crosses the wrong Vilarian, or if her mother sells her into indentured servitude.

"I know. And I want that to happen as little as you do."

"Is there anything we can do to help?" The question was a plea, and she hated herself for thinking of him as a prince instead of her husband, if only for a moment.

"Well—" Kresten hedged as he grabbed her hand. "I don't know. Maybe. Maybe not. At least they have food and the Fleet won't bother them in the future."

"That's huge," she admitted.

"You did that for them. And I love you for it."

If only her father did, too.

Kresten shook his head and glanced sideways at her. "I heard that. And you know what? I think we can work on that one—or at least clarify that I won't tolerate his rudeness as long as we're living in Therus. I know it doesn't completely solve anything, but it's a start."

"How do you plan on doing that? He hates you now too, Kresten. He won't agree to anything you ask."

He grinned. "Oh, I have some ideas. I think I'd like to meet with Governor Camden again—at his house this time."

CHAPTER SIX

It might have been perpetual summer on the coast, but the trees in the high mountains of Therus were a brilliant red and orange now. Kresten might have once claimed that he was an experienced interstellar traveler, but as Ryllis watched him, his eyes grew large at the warm leaves that fell from the trees. His beloved Kebnekaise Mountains were mostly pine, and the Vilarian capital scarcely had seasons at all. She'd always wondered if he'd visited Therus before now, and his surprise and wonder confirmed her suspicion that he had not.

She squeezed his hand tighter as the shuttle descended through the tops of the red and gold trees. Cipra's limestone buildings peeked through them—her father's house was on the small town's outskirts, and the forest too thick for their ship. Another shuttle with two Fleet security men followed behind as they descended toward Cipra's communal landing pad, its shadow covering the concrete. Ryllis tried not to think of it as an omen, but the hair on her forearms prickled as their shuttle came to a halt and the engines wound down.

"They're only here for a show of force," Kresten said, brushing his hand against her hair. "Need to make sure we won't have any issues getting to the house. Don't worry."

As if an attack was what she was worried about. She nodded at him, then closed her eyes against the all too familiar sight of the autumn trees outside. Kresten might fear whatever strange things lay within them, but the forest called to her. While the trees were thick and darkness prevailed in some of the densest areas, there was no threat. This was home.

Or was it? Vilaria was supposed to be home now.

She cracked her eyes again as the shuttle door was pulled open, then gasped as she peered outside.

"Kresten!"

Three large bobcats, as tall as her shoulders, stood harnessed to a lightweight sled with small wheels attached to the runners. The cats had been used for transportation in the mountains of Therus for hundreds of solar cycles, and though they preferred snow, more patient drivers could convince them to pull in other seasons—they were still cats, after all. Kresten had been cagey when she'd asked how he planned to get from town to the house, and here was the answer.

Kresten laughed. "Surprise. I borrowed them from a man in town. You like them?"

"Like?" She threw her hands around his neck and planted a kiss on his cheek. "I love it. It's so—so Cerethian."

"And it made you smile, so it's worth it. Truth be told, I'm terrified of riding along behind a bunch of cats, but I assume you can keep them from running us off a cliff. Come on—let's go say hello to these felines I'm trusting my life to."

Ryllis laughed and hopped out of the shuttle. The cats turned toward her as she approached, their feet darting about in small circles. She sunk her fingers into the velvet between the leader's ears, and the cat turned and let out a half purr, half snarl.

"All right, all right. You want to run, I get it. Better hop in," she said to Kresten, who was watching with wide eyes. "Seems like they've been hanging out here waiting on us a bit too long."

"Great. As long as they run and don't eat us."

Kresten climbed into the sled and waved a salute at the Fleet shuttle hovering above. It banked sharply, then settled down next to theirs. Ryllis gave each cat one last stroke and joined her husband. He drew the blanket from the floorboard over them and pulled her close, and she couldn't help laughing as she picked up the reins and whistled.

"Don't even think you can fool me," she said as the cats darted forward. "You're not cuddling—you're hanging on for dear life."

"Maybe so." He jabbed a finger in her ribs, and it only made her laugh harder, more than she had since they'd arrived on Cereth. It felt good. "But when they take me into a ravine, you're coming along for the ride."

"They won't." She gathered the reins in one hand and pointed ahead with her other, down the dirt road. "I'll correct them if they decide to get adventurous—besides, there aren't any ravines around here."

At that, he peered into the dense forest, and she felt his anxiety, even though the low rumble of a car followed them. *Security, everywhere.*

"It's a strange place for a governor to live," he told her, drawing her attention away from the trees.

"We lived a few streets away from the shuttle landing zone for a long time, but Zaella didn't enjoy living in town. She convinced him to move here. The Star Realm doesn't care where he works, and he's authorized a car."

"Ah. Zaella." He hesitated. "You don't sound like you minded too much."

"Would you? I barely remember the sea, and this is just as beautiful in its own way."

"And no one would notice if a few plants grew faster than the others."

"No," she whispered. "They wouldn't."

She'd been cautious, of course, but with an uncontrollable gift, it wasn't simple. Zaella's intense dislike of her made it easier, though—it wasn't as though her stepmother followed her around the property. As long as the chores were completed and Ryllis wasn't in the same room, the woman hadn't cared what she did.

The memories wound through her as the cats stopped at a fork in the road, sniffing and pawing at the ground. Ryllis flicked the reins, and they ground their feet into the dirt.

"What's with them?" Kresten asked.

"I don't know."

She flicked harder, then whistled again. The lead cat whined, then turned back toward her as their shadow car pulled up behind and stopped. Kresten hopped out and disappeared behind her to speak with Wikström and the other Shadow Force officer with him, one Captain Granqvist. She put her elbows on her knees and leaned forward. Something felt . . . wrong. The cats were nervous about something, but she couldn't decide what. It wasn't as though they had many predators.

Reluctantly, she pushed the warm blanket aside, jumped out, and paced around the sled. The cats watched her, but she ignored them, letting the feel of the forest soothe her soul. It wasn't the pine forest of Kresten's mountains, and maybe that was why she was so on edge. Maybe it was just the anticipation of seeing her father again. Maybe her powers were waning. Maybe putting her hand on a tree would help.

She wandered to the edge of the trail, toward a large maple, five times Kresten's height. Red-gold leaves floated slowly down from its canopy, though it probably had another full lunar cycle before it was completely bare. The leaves stopped falling as she dragged her fingers down its bark, and she sighed.

You don't have to stop dropping leaves on my account.

An icy breeze blew through her hair, and she shivered, despite the cloak she wore. There couldn't be snow on the way, but they *were* rather high up. It wouldn't be unknown so early in the season. The cats would be happy, but what if they got stuck, had to stay at her father's house?

That was silly, she told herself. They had a trained driving team, plus a car, plus a shuttle.

Ryllis turned back, but Kresten was lost in conversation with Wikström and Granqvist. Leaves crunched under her feet as she stepped farther into the woods, cautiously avoiding the few mushrooms that clung to the last remnants of summer. Any other time she'd have bent down to gather them, but a circle of aspens caught her eyes, bleached and white in the warmth of the maple forest.

She picked her way through the piles of yellow leaves underneath and stood in the center, looking up. Blue sky shone through the tops of the almost-bare trees; the aspens swayed and groaned in the wind, what might as well have been dark eyes in the white bark focused on her. It was odd she couldn't remember such a stand of trees, but it *had* been a while since she'd set foot on Cereth, hadn't it? The Vilarian voices drifted away as she peeled off a loose piece of bark, and she closed her eyes while the breeze and birds took their place. This was nature. This was peace. This was—

"Ryllis?"

Her eyes snapped open at the feminine voice.

Zaella was strolling into the circle of aspens, one perfectly groomed eyebrow arched. Thick hiking boots appeared to be the only concession to the surrounding woods—her indigo coat was tapestry patterned and trimmed with fur, her hair perfectly curled, like she was at a party at the palace on Vilaria and not a windswept mountain. Her eyebrow remained arched as she stared, and Ryllis shoved her hands in her pockets to stop their sudden shaking.

"Zaella. We were on our way to see Father, but the cats—" The cats what? Had stopped? Gotten frightened? It sounded ridiculous, but now that the aspens were staring at her, she felt some of the same.

"Yes." Zaella's voice was as young and musical as always. "He sent me to find the prince."

Ryllis cocked her head to the side. "He didn't let you take the car?"

"I prefer to walk."

"I—I see."

What else was there to say? Zaella had just spoke more words to her in thirty seconds than she had in the three solar cycles prior to Ryllis's arrest.

But you are a princess now, she told herself. *Even Zaella—especially Zaella—wants to make a good impression.*

"Is he nearby?" Zaella asked. That look was still on her face—the one that identified Ryllis as a stupid child. "Your husband?"

Ryllis backed toward the path and pointed. "This way."

Zaella shook her head. "That's all right. I'll go tell your father you're on the way."

"We may be a while."

"Right. The cats are giving you trouble." She tossed her curls over her shoulder and waved as she ambled out of the circle. "Well, you are Cerethian—I'm sure you'll get them to cooperate."

Zaella disappeared into the woods on the other side of the aspens, and Ryllis shook her head as she made her way to the sled. Kresten was waiting, an impatient look on his face. He grabbed her arm, and she flinched at his sudden, rough touch, so unusual for him.

"You disappeared. Don't do that again."

She pulled away and glared at him. "You were busy. I took the opportunity to stretch my legs."

"You could have gotten lost. Gotten us stuck in the snow. Made me late."

"Here? Hardly." Ryllis wanted to snort, though something told her that his concern was actually for her.

"Just don't do it again, do you hear me?" he barked. "The cats are ready—get in and drive them. There's snow coming, and I don't care to ride along in it."

Ryllis frowned at him as she did what he ordered. This wasn't Kresten, not this snarling, impatient man. Had Wikström said something to him? Given him bad news? It didn't excuse his words, but there had to be some explanation. Even when she'd been his slave, he'd never commanded her to do anything.

She snuck glances at him as the cats pulled them toward the trail's left fork. They were running now, and she scarcely had to put pressure on the reins, but Kresten's dour expression hadn't changed. She'd done something wrong, that much was clear. Was it the way she'd wandered off? He should know she knew these woods better than the ones around his lodge on Vilaria, and he'd never said a word about her ambling about there.

It had to be his unfamiliarity with the area and his fear of insurgents or wild animals or whatever. That had to be it. He'd spent an entire solar cycle on Cereth, yes, but since the prison she'd been confined in was on the other side of the planet, it made sense that he felt uncomfortable in Therus.

She glanced at him one more time, from under her eyelashes, and this time he grinned.

"I can see why you're willing to brave your father to come here."

Ryllis set her jaw. He was going to be kind now? That wasn't how this worked.

"That's funny," she replied, all desire for forgiveness forgotten, "because five minutes ago, you were telling me what a horrible, dangerous place it is."

Kresten's brow creased. "I was?"

Don't play games. "There," she said coolly, taking a step away and closing off her mind. "Just up ahead."

Camden's house wasn't small, and it wasn't as decrepit as Kresten had expected for a place in the middle of the wood, which made sense upon further reflection. They might be in the middle of the mountains, but the man was still a regional governor of the Star Realm. They paid him well, if only to remind him that his status and wealth could always be taken away, which had happened frequently in other locations, sometimes through no fault of the governor himself. After all, the populace needed reminding, too.

In any case, the Star Realm's money had financed a well-kept three-story brick cottage in the center of a large clearing. Gabled windows peered from under the roof, and well-manicured shrubbery lined the expansive front porch, which was decorated with pots of autumn flowers.

Ryllis pulled the cats to a stop in front of the fence surrounding the house, then hopped out and detached the harnesses. They butted at her hand. Her fingers sunk into their fur, and she gave them a slight smile. They, at least, had always understood what freedom was.

"You just let them go?" he asked.

"Yes." She tossed the leads in the sled and gave the leader a pat on his rump before he dashed into the woods, the others following. "They hunt."

"I see."

Kresten didn't know what else to say. Ryllis had been short with him ever since they'd stopped and he and Wikström had conversed about the rest of the route. That was as much of a surprise as the house—she had to be anxious about seeing her bastard father again. He could understand that. He missed the feel of her body pressed against his in the sled, but there would be no chance for that now, not until they made their way back to the villa. He wouldn't be rejected again.

Ryllis turned toward him, apprehension on her face, as Wikström's car pulled up behind them. He knew that look—her life had shifted again, and she didn't know how to respond, didn't know how to act. The desire to kiss her and tell her everything would be all right overcame him, but before he could move toward her, the front door opened, and a young woman came down the brick stairs.

She couldn't have been more than ten solar cycles older than Ryllis, with wavy black hair past her shoulders and a certain look of arrogance in the tilt of her lips. It was an odd way for a Cerethian to greet three Shadow Force officers and a princess of a Vilarian Star Realm, but it didn't mean anything. Likely she was hiding her nerves. He would be, if he were in her position. Or maybe his usual empathy was failing him, and he was wrong altogether.

"Captain Westermark." Her voice was as melodious as he'd expected. The form of address wasn't, but he was wearing a uniform, wasn't he? And any Cerethian would probably prefer meeting him as a Fleet officer than as a prince. Wouldn't they? She went on before he could figure it out. "I'm Zaella Camden."

Shock flooded through him. *This is your stepmother?* he asked Ryllis. *She's . . . young.*

Yes. Her reply was curt.

Well. Wasn't that interesting? If he had to guess, Zaella Camden looked just like Ryllis's mother must have, another lifetime ago, but he couldn't judge. He'd been married before Ryllis, hadn't he? He knew the pain of losing a spouse—it could make men, and probably women as well, narrow-minded in their selection of a new one.

He nodded. "Madam Camden. Governor Camden is still at the office?"

"Yes. And the children are out back."

He'd wondered about the girls. Ryllis had two younger stepsisters she rarely spoke of, and he'd always been curious. What must it have been like to grow up without a raucous group of children around? He couldn't imagine it. The palace might as well have been a festival some days.

Ryllis poked at his mind, but he ignored her. "Good. May we?"

Zaella nodded, and he followed her inside, Ryllis on his arm. An undercurrent of worry combined with annoyance fairly radiated from her, but that was nothing new since they'd arrived on Cereth. She would learn, and if she didn't . . .

He chose the sofa under the front window, and Ryllis settled next to him while Wikström and Granqvist disappeared to search the house. Zaella's discomfort at that was palpable, even with his limited empathy, but she didn't say a word as their footsteps echoed on the stairs. It was unlikely Camden kept anything related to the resistance here, but it was just as unlikely he'd be stashing it at the office.

And that was his actual mission, wasn't it? To arrest and interrogate Camden, then bring him to trial? Ryllis would be furious he'd lied to her, but her feelings on the matter . . . well, didn't matter.

Zaella set two cups of tea in front of them and chose the chair farthest away, in a corner under an oil lamp. Didn't they have power out here? Maybe not. He hadn't noticed any lines, and the house was even lacking the crystals that powered the lights in his own properties. Maybe that was a conscious decision. He hadn't spent enough time on Cereth to know.

"Tavis told me what happened." Zaella crossed her legs. "After she was arrested."

"Did my father tell you he was the one who turned me in?" Ryllis's voice was acerbic.

"He didn't have a choice. You know that. What if you'd been guilty, and he had said nothing about it? They could have executed him."

"Madam Camden, I saw some of the evidence against Ryllis, and it looked damning enough. I'm curious—did he mention where he'd gotten it, why he was so convinced she was part of the resistance movement? Did someone else give him the information? Was he protecting someone?"

Zaella tossed her curls. "I don't know."

"He must have mentioned something to you. Something he neglected to tell the Fleet. Not on purpose, certainly, but . . ."

It didn't feel like the woman was lying, but there was a strange murkiness about her emotions. For the second time, he felt a dash of fear that perhaps his empathy *was* fading. But why?

"He loves her." Zaella shrugged. "Turning her in before they harmed her was better than letting her die in a raid. He wouldn't have made those accusations otherwise."

She's lying, Ryllis broke in.

He wanted to sigh at the interruption.

"Zaella," Ryllis asked, "if my father is in town, why did you tell me he had sent you to find us?"

The woman's hands fluttered, then settled on the arm of her chair. "I misspoke."

No one was this bad at lying. Surely Camden had told her what her guest did for a living? Odds were she thought she could outwit a fool prince of the Star Realm and failed telepath, but they'd see about that. This Zaella woman would look as good as the governor with a few black circles on her arm, and he wouldn't mind passing out and then waking up with a headache if it meant he got the truth out of her.

Ryllis reached for her tea, then drew back. He felt her nearness, felt how much she wanted to touch him, but etiquette demanded she stay a safe distance away. He'd let her know how poorly she'd behaved if she didn't.

He startled. Where had that thought come from? He'd promised Ryllis he'd never hurt her, and he'd meant it, more than he cared about his own life. It was the darkness brewing outside, the forecasted storm Wikström had warned him about, had to be. That and his anxiety about confronting Camden again were messing with his mind. He brushed his fingers against hers, no matter how inappropriate the move might be, and she touched her fingertips to his.

Zaella frowned at the gesture and shifted in her chair as footsteps echoed on the porch outside. Beside him, Ryllis inhaled sharply, but he didn't have a chance to tell her to grow a backbone before Camden appeared in the doorway. The governor's cheeks turned red, and Kresten stood.

"This isn't a social visit this time, Governor."

Ryllis tensed, but Camden looked him up and down, no less furious. "It certainly appears to be one."

I shouldn't have brought Ryllis, Kresten said to himself.

He brushed his thought away almost immediately. They'd

agreed her presence was the best way to keep Camden off guard, so why was he second-guessing himself now? The murkiness swelled, and he clenched his jaw, then glanced up the stairs as Wikström and Granqvist came down, drawing Camden's attention.

"You searched my house?"

"Yes. Under the authority of Colonel Berglund, Commander, Therus Station." Kresten forced a bored tone into his voice. "You may file a complaint if you wish."

"You are only harassing me because you believe that traitor"—Camden jabbed a finger in Ryllis's direction—"over a man who has faithfully served the emperor for over twenty solar cycles! You're biased. She's gotten into your mind, too."

Wikström handed Kresten a data disk, and he shoved it in his pocket.

"What is that?" Camden demanded. "You can't—"

"If the lieutenant thought it was worth looking into further, I certainly can." He jerked his head at Wikström. "Get him out of here."

CHAPTER SEVEN

*R*yllis tried to whistle for the cats one more time, but between the noise of the wind in the trees and her own anguish, it was a lost cause. Whether the impending storm was hiding her call or her voice sounded broken to the cats or the woods didn't matter. Except for the swaying of the trees, the forest into which they'd disappeared to earlier remained still. Even Bry and Greta had fled inside. She'd wanted to speak to Bry especially, but her stepsister had given her an odd look when she'd approached them in the barnyard, so she'd backed off. They'd grown up but still avoided her, and along with Kresten's odd behavior, it was too much rejection to handle. Tears gathered, and she leaned her forehead against the back of the sled and closed her eyes.

Kresten had lied.

He'd known exactly why his father had sent him back to Cereth, and he'd lied to her about it. *About her own father!* And he'd expected her to . . . what? To simply look pretty and act unquestioningly, even if she disagreed with his decisions? How was that any different from being a slave? Could he possibly understand if she tried to explain? Or even let him into her mind? Her fists clenched until her knuckles grew sore. Well, that was something she wouldn't be doing anytime soon. He didn't deserve the intimacy.

Kresten's boots crunched on the dried leaves and acorns behind her, and she stiffened, then wiped her face with a chilled palm. His earlier mood made sense now. Everything made sense now. He'd hidden things from her before, his telepathic skills being the most important, though she'd always had the sense that being less than honest with her—being less than honest with everyone he came across, truthfully—was painful for him. Still, this was unforgiveable.

"Snow's moving in," he called out from behind her. "We're spending the night."

Ryllis spun around, her breath visible in the icy air. "Why? Snow's never stopped the cats before."

Kresten prodded at her mind, and she closed him off. He could use his voice if he wanted to talk. Telepathy was too personal. After his betrayal over her father, she needed to stay guarded. He couldn't hurt her again if she was.

"First, you lost the cats," he said out loud, pointing at the forest. "Even if you hadn't, Lieutenant Wikström took the car."

"I didn't lose anything!" Her stomach twisted. The cats were trained and should have returned. "They'll be back. They're just eating or maybe—"

"Or what? Unless they're back in the next thirty seconds, their return won't help anything. That trail will be mud soon. Tomorrow, once it dries out, or it snows enough to cover the trail, we'll head back to town."

"Why can't we take my father's car?"

Kresten didn't blink, and she ground her feet into the dried dirt. Staying here with Zaella was out of the question, but he was right. The cats couldn't pull the sled in the mud. If enough snow fell, they could remove the wheels and make it a sleigh, but heading out in a storm was just asking to get stuck. And getting stuck out on the trail with Kresten, after he had lied and the way he was acting now, was even more out of the question.

"Then I'd like to stay in the barn out back," she said.

"The barn?" Kresten's lip curled, and she almost laughed at his reaction, but she stopped herself before she could show any amusement. Nothing Kresten did now was funny. Nothing could make her smile.

"Zaella used to have a hired man help around here, but he moved on a long time ago. There's a small room in the loft where he used to live—I used to go up there and hide when I couldn't stand things anymore. It's comfortable."

"No. Absolutely not. You're not staying in a barn."

"What's the matter, Your Highness? Is a barn beneath you?" It was cruel perhaps, but she hadn't been able to stop herself.

"Ryllis, stop." His plea should have been accompanied by a touch, but he simply stood there, arms folded. *This isn't like you.*

His voice in her mind made her jump; she'd dropped her shield again. Flustered, she tried to block out his presence once more, but keeping herself from crying took all her excess energy. She couldn't cry in front of Zaella. Fine, then. He could speak to her mind all he wanted. She wouldn't do the same in return.

"This isn't like me? I don't think you have any idea what you're talking about." She wanted to scream at him, but Zaella would hear. "This is exactly like me, and you know it. You're the one who's acting like a stranger. You lied and you—"

Listen, there are things—

He broke off, and Ryllis looked up. Zaella was marching across the lawn, a shawl around her shoulders and her arms wrapped around her chest.

"It's going to get bad soon, Captain Westermark." There wasn't a hint of fear in her voice, which was odd for someone who'd just watched her husband arrested. "Why don't you come inside and get comfortable?"

Kresten sighed. "We'll do that," he said, even though it was perfectly clear to Ryllis that Zaella had meant him and him only. He held out his hand at long last. "Let's go, Ryllis."

One raindrop hit her nose, and she shivered. "You stay in the house with Zaella and the girls. I'll be in the barn."

Kresten shouted her name, first out loud and then several times in her head, but she stormed around the side of the house before he could do anything else.

The ladder to the loft was as decrepit as it'd always been, but when Ryllis peered over the edge of the old attic, she almost fell off the rung in shock. Alderson, the handyman, had vocally resisted any kind of luxury for himself, preferring to save his credits for liquor, but gone was the dirty mattress on the floor of the utilitarian loft and the stacks of hay he'd used as tables. In their place lay a brocade wool rug with a new bed on top. The linens looked expensive and smelled fresh—much fresher than the rest of the barn downstairs. Shelves had been built into the far wall, next to the window which held new glass, and the books appeared to be dry. Alderson had never been one to care about the small cracks between the beams, so someone had to have filled them.

Even if it'd been Zaella, in that very second, Ryllis didn't care. She flopped on top of the silk coverlet and stared up at the ceiling, now painted a soft brown. Rain lashed at the window, and she flinched as the trees joined it. It would get cold soon. It always did when storms like this hit the mountains. Perhaps flouncing out to the barn had been a bad idea, for the house was much warmer and had indoor plumbing, but she simply couldn't face Kresten. Not now.

Shadow Force had taken her father, and there was no way out for him. She hated him, resented him, should be thrilled he was getting to experience the horror she'd gone through after she'd been arrested, but he was family. He was Cerethian, and therefore she would always be on his side, no matter what he'd done to her or Kresten's family or the Star Realm. Even if she hated him. She should be able to celebrate him being gone and tormented by the Fleet, not lay here and be so conflicted. So why couldn't she? Why did witnessing her father's arrest continue to haunt her? Would she ever be able to forget?

With a shiver, she pushed herself to her feet and explored the rest of the loft, more to keep warm than out of actual curiosity. It turned out there was running water, even if it was only a small toilet and handheld shower behind a curtain in the corner. A small cactus sat on the ledge by the window there, and she picked it up and ran her fingers over the spines. Whoever had placed it there had likely thought the humidity from the shower and sink was enough, but it was shriveled, so she gave it a drink and brought it back out to the main room.

Between the lingering twilight and incoming storm, it was

dark now, and while there might be water, there wasn't power. No surprise there, since the Star Realm controlled new power connections just like they controlled everything else—even in a regional governor's house. But there was a large basket filled with candles, and she picked out a few, Kresten's dislike for them at the front of her mind. He said they were dangerous, but all Cerethians knew candle safety from near-birth. It was the only reliable light sometimes. She lit three and placed them in the fluted glass globes on the table. A small film of gel on the bottom would extinguish the flame if they tipped over.

That completed, she collapsed on the bed and closed her eyes. Exploring her home for the evening hadn't done enough to take her mind off things. Kresten was no doubt still angry she'd stayed in the barn instead of the house, but she couldn't be around Zaella. She might play the dutiful governor's wife and loyal Star Realm subject around him, but it had to be an act. At the very least, it was ingratiating. How couldn't he see it? He'd never been one to surround himself with sycophants.

But then, Kresten had never seen how Zaella had treated her. While Bry and Greta dined on roast chicken, Ryllis had been forced to content herself with whatever was left in the pantry— whatever Zaella approved of her taking, of course. Greta had been allowed music lessons, an almost unheard extravagance in rural Therus, but when Ryllis had asked for a small doll at only ten solar cycles old, Zaella had laughed at her. *As if we have the finances for that kind of indulgence,* she'd said. Rose had been lucky to be old enough to find her own way through life.

Then came the lack of schooling—the only thing her father had stood up to Zaella about—the smacks on her palm with a stick when she was caught sneaking food, and the housework. Oh, the endless housework. Bry and Greta had kept their distance shortly after moving in, spurred on by Zaella's constant claims of how Ryllis was an unsuitable companion for them. Whether she was accusing Ryllis of seducing Alderson or stealing food or enchanting the cow into producing less milk, her allegations were constant and creative.

It was enough to make one wonder if Zaella had known about her powers back then.

No matter. No one could harm her for helping the little cactus now, and as Ryllis picked it up and gently placed her hands on it again, she saw it had already perked up. She held it in front of her lips and pursed them. It was silly to show gratitude toward a plant, but she'd feel much worse if it wasn't up here, wouldn't she? There was no reason not to thank it for keeping her company when her own husband refused to.

"Did you just kiss a cactus?"

The cactus hit the floor as she jerked toward the voice, spilling dirt all over the rug. Kresten's head stuck over the top of the ladder, a bemused look on his face. His hair was drenched, and Ryllis doubted the rest of him had fared much better.

"Maybe." She brushed the dirt into a pile and tried to shove it back in the pot, a futile effort around the spines. "What do you want?"

"I want to see how my wife is doing."

He pulled himself the rest of the way up, leaving a small puddle where he stood, and she tried not to admire how effortlessly he'd flung himself off the ladder.

"You certainly didn't seem to care before," she snapped at him.

"I—" Kresten wiped the water from his head and knelt next to her, brushing the rest of the dirt from the rug. "I don't know what you're talking about. You've been so angry with me, and it's not just because of your father. You've been upset with me since before we arrived at the house."

"And you've been rude." She replaced the cactus on the table and perched on the bed, challenging him to disagree.

"Rude?" The crease between his eyes grew deeper. "Darling star, I don't remember being rude. I know you're on edge, I can't imagine how difficult this must be for you, so I'm trying to make this as easy as I can. I wouldn't have been rude."

He sounded baffled. Perhaps he was stressed and overworked and couldn't remember the things he'd said and done, but that was no excuse. Still, as a violent shiver worked its way from his head to his feet, her emotions thawed a bit.

"Well, you were," she said. "How could you not realize it? You're not acting like someone who's trying to make a single thing easier. But go take a hot shower before you freeze to death, and we can talk about it some more. It's behind the curtain."

Kresten glanced at the makeshift bathroom. *No plans to join me?*

She froze at his teasing tone. An overture, perhaps? Well, not one she'd accept soon. "No. This one is medicinal. Get warmed up, then we'll discuss it."

He winked at her as he stripped off his sodden shirt and headed behind the curtain. Water splashed behind it, noisy even over the rain outside, and she leaned her head against the headboard.

I love you.

The declaration shouldn't have startled her, but it did, so much she couldn't give him the expected response.

Why, Kresten? Why didn't you tell me? I wouldn't have said anything to him, but just knowing would have made things easier. If making this easier was what you really wanted for me, there were so many ways you could have gone about this.

I explained before. I couldn't say anything—you know that. Shadow Force business is kept close, even—especially when it involves family.

She was quiet for a moment, watching the steam rise over the curtain in wisps of fog that matched the weather outside. What he said was true enough, and deep down, the way he'd handled things hadn't surprised her, but it didn't make things any better.

Do you really think he's guilty, Kresten?

Kresten's sigh wasn't audible over the thunder and shower,

but judging by his pause, he was doing just that—or trying to decide what to say. The attic was silent for a long while except for the pounding of rain on the roof and the wind howling through the eaves.

I don't know. I pray he's not, but Ryllis, judging by what little they told me before they headed back to town, it doesn't look good.

It didn't look good for me either, she reminded him.

Another pause. *True.*

Will the Fleet release him if he's found innocent? Will he be able to resume his duties?

It seemed important somehow that he would, even though she could never explain why to Kresten. Maybe it was just the hope that a few Cerethians still held a bit of their own future in their hands. Maybe it was hope Father would one day change his mind, love her again, treat her as his daughter. Silly, stupid hopes.

I suppose that depends.

On?

Ryllis . . .

On what?

On how it looks, I suppose. It would undermine our authority here if we allowed someone under suspicion to continue his governorship. His Majesty would never allow that—especially with the insurgencies and protests that have plagued us forever. That protects Cereth too, you know. A violent rebellion with no chance of success hurts everyone.

Ryllis stared out the window. She could read between the lines—even if the Star Realm cleared him, they would never trust him again. And, it followed, neither would she. If she thought the way the nobles in Carilles had treated her before was terrible, things would only get worse after this. A former slave, a onetime prisoner—yes, they grudgingly accepted her new position in Vilarian court life, if only because the emperor ordered it. He would never order the same regarding her father's crimes.

Do you think he's guilty? she finally asked.

The water cut off, and Kresten appeared on the other side of the curtain, a towel around his waist.

"I'm not sure," he said, shaking his short hair dry. "I certainly hope not, but he was certainly convinced of your guilt, enough to provide some rather damning evidence. Why would he have done that if he wasn't protecting himself? I know you said your relationship was strained, but no one hates their own children that much. I simply can't imagine any other reason for it."

"I know." Her shoulders sagged. "You're going to freeze if you stand there like that before your clothes dry, you know." Too late, she realized she'd issued an invitation.

"Too true." He tossed the towel back onto the bathroom floor and pulled back the coverlet from underneath her. "Only one solution for that at this point."

Ryllis couldn't contain her laugh that time. "What am I supposed to do with you? You're absolutely hopeless."

He hopped into the bed and grabbed her by the waist. "But you love me, anyway."

She turned her head away, ashamed she'd let her guard down. "You lied to me. And on the way here, you were so unkind. And Kresten, I just don't know . . ."

He pulled her closer as another crash of thunder shook the barn. "I honestly don't remember being so, and if I was, I apologize. But are you sure you aren't imagining things?"

She hadn't imagined it. There was no way she made any of it up. She'd never been given to flights of fancy, even under stress. But as she curled up next to him and he twisted her hair around his fingers, loving and kind, she couldn't help thinking that maybe she had.

CHAPTER EIGHT

Kresten woke to the sound of silence. It wasn't an unfamiliar feeling, since it was a sensation he felt every time he was through questioning a prisoner, and to a lesser extent when Ryllis blocked him from her mind, but this was different. This wasn't lonely. It was comforting and paradoxically warm, like a cozy blanket or much-needed fire. He rolled over and looked around for the source of the silence, but he didn't need to see outside to know where it'd come from.

Snow.

Ryllis didn't stir as he sat up and quietly headed to the window. They'd lain awake, holding each other, listening to the thunder, which must have transitioned to snow after they'd fallen asleep. A thick carpet of it covered the ground and clung to the red leaves that remained on the trees, and certainly the cats would have no trouble dragging the sleigh back into town. He couldn't wait to hop in the sleigh with Ryllis, bury themselves in blankets, and hold on to each other the whole way back. After yesterday, they needed the time together. She needed to be reminded how much he loved her, and he needed to be reminded how much she needed him. It would be perfect.

As he stared out the window, Kresten realized it didn't matter that the barn wasn't connected to the power grid, since the snow would have likely taken out the lines, anyway. He squinted toward the main house, but no lights showed through the trees. Yes, the snow had been heavy, just like fall in the Kebnekaises. It made this foreign, not-quite-enemy planet feel like home, and a strange feeling of melancholy washed over him as he watched the flurries slow, then finally stop.

Silently, he padded to the bathroom and checked on his uniform. It was dry, if a little chilled, and he shivered as he dressed. Ryllis would have a harder time in the dress she'd worn the day before, but if he could talk her into stepping foot in the main house again, she'd warm up quickly. The fireplaces would certainly be blazing by now, and he'd bury her in blankets for the ride back into town. The only question was—had she forgiven him enough to let him help her? He was almost afraid to find out.

Still unwilling to disturb her sleep, he pried himself from the view out the window and took a look around the loft. The candles had long since gone out, but a thin beam of sunlight broke through the trees and scattered to the old wood floor. Had Ryllis escaped up here when her stepmother had been especially horrible? He wanted to lay into the woman for what she'd done to her, but maybe it didn't matter this many solar cycles later. Ryllis was safe and living a better life than Zaella Camden could ever dream of.

Not that the woman was all that deprived. He'd visited poorer areas of Cereth—of Therus itself—and she was living about as well as possible. The loft had clearly been redone, and the book-case against the wall was filled with more books than he'd seen outside of an imperial library. Even on Vilaria, the old classics were scarce. He picked one up and blew the dust off the cover, suppressing a sneeze.

THERUS WILD PLANTS & NATURAL AREAS/MOUN-TAINS, the cover read. More dust flew as he turned through pages and pages of flower illustrations and tree identification. It looked like something Ryllis would have enjoyed—would still enjoy. He knew he was just imagining the past, but he couldn't help thinking that it'd been hers and her stepmother had taken it. He flipped another few pages and squinted at the handwritten notes.

Yes, there it was, clear as the night sky—Ryllis's handwriting. He set it aside, pondering, and reached for the one next to it, one that seemed oddly dust-free. Well-read, perhaps? He didn't recognize the language, which was strange in an empire where everyone finally spoke the same one, but some people considered books collectibles. He scanned the pages, stopping when he came upon a hand-drawn illustration that was almost identical to the circle of aspens on the way up the trail.

Even stranger.

He traced his finger on the words underneath. Even the alphabet was different, curved and circular. An ancient local language? He didn't know enough about Cereth's history and regions to know. Maybe Ryllis would, but he hated to ask her anything that would dredge up bad memories. She hurt enough as it was. He skimmed through the rest of the book, but none of the other illustrations were familiar.

Racking his brain wouldn't help. For the first time, he felt out of his element, like he was missing something or making the situation out to be something it wasn't. Maybe it was a natural phenomenon in this area. Clonal trees grew in concentric circles in some parts of Vilaria, after all. Nature was beautiful and mathematical all at once, and someone like him had no chance of ever understanding it.

"You're up already."

He turned. Ryllis was making her way to the bookcase beside him, the blanket around her shoulders and trailing on the floor behind her.

"Yeah. Couldn't sleep." He set the book back in its place, wound his arms around her waist, and touched his lips to hers. "You warm enough?"

"Getting used to it." She scooted next to him, wrapped the blanket around them both, and laid her head on his shoulder. Maybe she was close to forgiving him. "I grew up here, remember. It was always colder than I would have preferred in the winter."

And Ryllis, he knew, didn't deal with snow well. That paradox was yet another of her charms. "The good news is," he said, "there looks to be enough snow to use the sleigh to get back."

"But the cats . . ." Ryllis looked up at him, worry in her expression. "What if they haven't come back? What if they don't?"

"They'll come around, right? You said so yourself. But before you even try calling for them again, you need something to eat and something much warmer to wear. Feel like trying for the main house?"

The worry turned to something worse.

I don't want to be around her, she said. *I don't want to be there.*

"Ok. That's all right. I understand." He brushed her cheek with his fingers. If she was speaking telepathically, it meant she didn't trust her own voice. "How about I go in and find you some warmer clothes and breakfast?"

"Loan me clothes? Zaella will never agree to that."

He laughed in her mind, though he could feel that his expression was anything but amused. *You've forgotten who I am. She may put up a fight, but I'll win in the end.*

That drew a small smile. *I almost feel sorry for that woman, not knowing what kind of trouble's headed her way. Don't go easy on her.*

He gave her another quick kiss—anything more would keep him here much too long—and swung himself down the ladder. The main barn was freezing, but there in the corner lay three tawny balls, sound asleep in one dangerous heap of teeth and claws. Kresten whistled in their direction. One perked up to yawn, then lay its head back down again. He didn't dare disturb them further lest they use those teeth on him; he simply gritted his own and pulled the barn open.

A blast of blown snow hit his face as he stepped into the drift just outside. Thankfully his boots were waterproof, so he tromped through the yard in snow up to his knees, then pounded on the back door of the house. A young girl around sixteen solar cycles admitted him without a word, and he shook off the remaining snow on the sunken floor. The owner of this particular house might hate his Ryllis, but the Star Realm had trained him too well for him to track water and mud across her floor. Etiquette and protocol could be so tiring.

"Greta?" he guessed. The Cerethian custom of nicknames was the opposite of what he was used to, but calling her Margaret was out of the question for now. Full names were for family, too intimate for strangers to use.

"Yes, Your Highness." She ran her hair through her blonde waves as her eyes flitted away from his uniform. "My mother is waiting for you in the kitchen. Breakfast is almost ready."

"It smells good. But first, Ryllis needs some clothes, if you would. A coat, at least. It's going to be a long way back to town, and we simply weren't prepared for the weather."

Greta nodded. "I can probably find you something upstairs, sir. If you'd follow me."

"Does she have any belongings here still?" he asked as he followed her light footsteps up the stairs. "I can send someone for the rest of them if there are."

"I don't think so, sir. Mother threw them away when she left."

When she left. Such a polite way of saying *when she was arrested and forced into slavery for something she hadn't even done.* He wanted to strike out at someone, anyone, but he clenched his fists at his side and moved on.

"I found a book in the barn loft that had her handwriting in it. Do you think your mother would mind if we took it with us? I suspect Ryllis would love to have a small part of her past back."

The girl swung around as she stepped onto the top landing, her eyes wide. "You went through the books in the loft, Your Highness?"

Interesting. That had worried her, and it made him desperate to get back to Ryllis and the strange book he'd found next to hers.

"No," he lied. "Not really. Just pulled a few out and skimmed through them, but reading has never been a great hobby of mine."

Greta exhaled. "She doesn't like people messing with her things. She grew up poor, and I suppose she still feels vulnerable somehow, like this life will be taken from her as well. Maybe it has been."

Kresten would have thought a woman who'd had a terrible childhood would have been kinder to her stepdaughter, but that wasn't an argument to have with a child. He stood back while Greta dug through a trunk in what appeared to be a spare room —he wasn't ignorant enough to not realize it'd been Ryllis's at one point in time—then nodded his approval at the emerald cloak she pulled out. It looked like nothing more than a bunch of green fabric to him, but Ryllis would adore it, that much he knew.

He tossed the heavy fabric over his arm and followed Greta back down the hallway. The scent of eggs drifted up from downstairs, and his mouth watered as he put his foot on the top step. They wouldn't be as good as his housekeeper's, but anything familiar on this planet was something worth rushing for. His knee buckled as he took another step, and he barely caught himself on the handrail as yesterday's murkiness wrapped itself around him again.

What in the Realm?

"Are you all right, Your Highness?" Greta must have sensed he wasn't right behind her anymore, for she turned, her eyes creased. "The stairs are old. Please watch your step."

"Lost my balance." He tried to shake off the darkness, but it clung to him like a fine mist, though moving was easier now. "My fault."

She pursed her lips and continued downstairs into the kitchen, where Zaella was standing in front of a wood stove. Kresten tossed the cloak to a chair and cleared his throat. It did nothing to dispel that fog that still hung around him. Maybe it was the fireplace. Compared to his hike across the yard, the room was hot and oppressive. Yes, that was it.

"How did you fare last night, Captain Westermark?" Zaella

asked. "I told you it would be chilly in the barn—I told you it would have been best for you to stay here."

"I was fine." He'd been about to say *we*, then stopped. Ryllis had run out to the barn of her own free will. What did he care if she'd been cold last night?

Zaella turned back to the stove. "You may as well stay here and warm up while you eat breakfast, yes?"

It was as good a plan as any. Kresten knocked the cloak to the floor and took its place as Greta set a cup of coffee in front of him. It smelled . . . there wasn't a suitable enough word in the Realm to describe how lovely it smelled. Much better than the swill Ryllis made, that was certain. Eggs and some sort of Cerethian fried meat followed the coffee, and he was swiping his plate with a thick piece of bread when a Fleet snow crawler pulled to a halt outside.

The elder of Ryllis's stepsisters, Bry—who'd spent the entirety of breakfast whispering at her sister—jumped up to let Wikström and Granqvist in the back door. If any of the Camden women were anxious at the appearance of more Fleet personnel so soon after Camden's arrest, they didn't show it. Except maybe Zaella, who downed a third cup of coffee while they shook the snow off their coats. If Kresten didn't know better, he'd guess she was trying to fit in one last cup before they took her away, too. But he'd never let that happen. Zaella was innocent of everything. He was certain of that now, more certain than he'd ever been of anything in his life.

"Where is Her Highness?" Granqvist asked.

"Uh—" Kresten glanced around the now-crowded kitchen. "The barn."

Wikström raised his eyebrows. "The barn, sir?"

"She's being petty about having to stay here last night." When Wikström's brows remained raised, Kresten had the fleeting sensation he'd said something wrong. "Never mind. I'll go get her."

He threw his coat back on, then stomped back to the barn through the drifts in the yard. The bobcats were up and about this time, whining and pacing through bags of something he didn't want to guess at. He held out his hand in a kind of reminder that they'd get on the road soon, but he didn't dare get any closer before scaling the ladder to the loft.

Ryllis was huddled in bed, an extra blanket around her, paging through the book of plant identification. She looked up at him and smiled, then frowned at his empty hands.

"No coat?" she asked. Her eyes fell. "I knew she wouldn't agree to give you one."

Blast it. He'd forgotten the cloak. And breakfast for her. How? He scarcely remembered what he'd done in the house, but he'd been gone from the barn long enough for the rising sun to shift to the center of the loft.

He shook his head. "Ryllis—I forgot it. I'm sorry. Something just came over me, and I—I must be exhausted. I don't know what's going on."

"Oh, no. I should have known." She hopped out of bed and put her arms around him. "Is this related to your blackouts?"

The blackouts.

He hadn't thought of them in almost a solar cycle, but yes, that had to be it. It was one reason he'd resigned from the Fleet, after all. After every telepathic interrogation he'd run, some more effective than others, he'd ended up unconscious. Sometimes for minutes, sometimes for hours. Fatigue, the Shadow Force medical personnel had claimed, but they'd never looked into it past the briefest of examinations. No, they didn't care, not when they didn't have to deal with the wretchedness and humiliation of passing out in front of their colleagues—not to mention prisoners.

And now his father expected him to interrogate Ryllis's father, and soon, regardless of the cost to his body and marriage. That had to be what was wrong with him. The stress alone was enough to make the hardest man crack.

"Probably. Yes." He sighed. "I feel like I'm living in a fog lately, wandering through a mist that's taken over my mind. It's different from my blackouts, too, but I can't explain why."

"You need to see a doctor." She ran a palm across his forehead, then kissed his cheek. "Soon. If I arrange for something when we get back to Epuas, will you cooperate?"

Kresten burst into laughter. "You know me too well, darling star. Yes. I'll see a doctor. Whatever they want to do, I'll agree to it. Just give me a few days, will you? Things are going to be busy for a while."

Ryllis dropped her hands to her sides and her eyes to the floor. "I understand."

"Do you?" He lifted her chin, but she forced her gaze away.

"I would rather think so, having been through it not so long ago."

"This wasn't my idea, Ryllis."

"You don't need to keep saying it." She paced back to the bed and pulled the blanket around herself. "I know whose fault this is."

"I'll keep saying it until you're not angry with me anymore."

"You ordered my father's arrest, Kresten! How in the Realm am I supposed to be anything but angry with you?"

"I didn't order it." Kresten clenched his fists. Ryllis knew. She hadn't been there in that throne room when the emperor had ordered it of him, but she knew how things had gone. She had to. Arguing with her, upsetting her more, it wasn't worth it. Either Camden was innocent and the entire situation would blow over in a few lunar cycles, or he was guilty, and Realm's sake, he didn't want to imagine what that meant for Ryllis. She was safe—she would be safe if he had to disappear and take her with him—but emotionally? No, she would be the last thing from fine, and would be for a long time.

"Then be angry. I probably deserve it."

She flinched at that. "Are we going back to the villa? It's stopped snowing, and the bobcats have been whining to run so loudly that I can barely hear myself think."

"Yes." His answer was clipped. "But Lieutenant Wikström brought a snow crawler if you'd prefer."

"I would not prefer." Then she added, *I don't want to stay here any longer.*

Kresten inclined his head.

"Someone needs to return to the team to town, anyway." She tossed her hair. "You'll have plenty of time to practice your apologies on the shuttle back to the villa, so best get thinking."

"Might I practice them on the way into town as well?"

Ryllis's mouth opened, then shut. "I—"

He shrugged. "I need lots of practice. But if you'd rather I stumble along, then by all means . . ."

"I'll make you a deal," she said. "Go find that coat, and help me harness up the cats and remove the wheels, and you can work on your apologizing while you keep me warm in the sleigh."

"Is that all?"

"No." Ryllis picked up the book and threw it at his chest. He caught it one-handed, and she laughed. "Pack my book in there while you're at it."

"Deal," he said.

CHAPTER NINE

This situation was exactly what Kresten had wanted to avoid when he'd written his letter of resignation from the Fleet last solar cycle on Vilaria. All of it. The bureaucracy, the frustration, the trying to condemn a man who might very well be innocent—and the Star Realm, naturally, cared more about making a point than protecting the innocent. Camden would be a perfect example, proof that no one was safe, not even someone appointed by the emperor himself.

A threat.

And he was through with threats.

He was through with all of it, and he didn't care who knew any longer.

Berglund had been watching him pace back and forth across the empty office down the hall from Camden's cell for the past five minutes, but he hadn't said a word. Even a Fleet colonel wouldn't interrupt the thought process of a Shadow Force man, though Kresten was at least half a lunar cycle from trying telepathy on a new prisoner. Traditional techniques first, always.

No one was ever entirely certain how long a telepath had, but some fell silent after ten solar cycles, some fifteen. It was the very rare telepath indeed who made it more than seventeen, and those were the ones who always had a light schedule—which he did not. After all, his tough interrogation schedule was what the medical people had said caused his blackouts, and he wasn't looking forward to the next one.

On the other hand, if he kept collapsing, maybe the emperor would come to his senses and rescind these ridiculous orders. But that would be too easy, wouldn't it?

"I think there's been some sort of mistake." He'd been thinking of his father, of Shadow Force, but the words flew out of his mouth as he stared at the copy of Camden's calendar that was projected on the wall. His brain caught up with his statement almost immediately. "I—something's wrong here."

"Some mistake?" Doubt laced Berglund's words. "What kind? Mine, yours, or his?"

Kresten wanted to bash his own head against the wall, but he wouldn't subject himself to that kind of headache until and unless Camden had those nice circles on his arm. No sense in pain for pain's sake.

"I don't know, sir." It was an inadequate answer, and he hurried on to cover it up, even though he didn't technically report to Berglund. "Camden's not stupid enough to have a secondary calendar with resistance meetings on it. No one's that chancy. Especially in his position. He's smart. He's got connections. He—"

He what, though? It was a question he truly had no answer to, at least not now.

"It's possible he thought his position would protect him," Berglund said. "It's happened before."

Through the mental fog that had never quite left him alone, Kresten sighed. The colonel was probably right. This sort of thing happened all the time with high-ranking Fleet officers and imperial-appointed bureaucrats. They never learned. They all thought they were safe, and that couldn't be further from the truth. Whether it was treason or simply taking a bit of the Star Realm's money for themselves, the facts always came out in the end.

"Possibly," he admitted. "I suppose he's arrogant enough to believe we'd never come after him."

"And there are three others living in that house."

"Two of them are practically children, and the calendar is male handwriting. The analysts conclusively matched it to Camden's. It wasn't as though they didn't have enough samples to go through." No, everything from his office in town and at his house had been confiscated and compared to communiqués that Camden had previously sent to Vilaria. "The analysts are certain it's not one of the others."

Unless someone was trying to frame Camden . . .

He slapped the thought down. There was no time to come up with foolish ideas that couldn't possibly turn out to be true. His Imperial Majesty had told him to investigate Camden, and that was just what he would do—unless there was obvious evidence to the contrary. By the Realm, he didn't want to be the one to tell the Fleet that someone else appeared to be guilty of what Camden had been accused of.

"Children have been involved in insurgencies." Berglund peered at him oddly. "Maybe not so frequently in Therus, but it's happened on Cereth before. And even if you truly believe the children are innocent, there's always Camden's wife. She sees things most Cerethians don't. Perhaps she's fed up with us."

"She seems loyal." *And I sound naïve.* "But Shadow Force will of course question her as well. Not here," he added quickly, without knowing why. "I think she'd react better if we keep her off guard —if she believes she's completely safe from prosecution."

"Ah. Well, you know better how to handle these situations than I do. I'm glad it's Shadow Force's mess and not mine." Berglund glanced at his chronometer, then grabbed his untouched cup of tea. "I've got a meeting in five. Any other support you need, let me know. The full strength of Therus Station is at your disposal."

Kresten murmured a goodbye and flopped back in his chair, only to stare at the calendar. Putting pieces of a broken vase together was exhausting, and gluing them so they didn't fall apart even more so. Especially when he had to make the glue himself. Still, imperial orders were imperial orders, and it was better than confronting Camden, so he sat there in this chilled concrete box in Ryllis's former homeland, puzzling over things he hadn't a clue about.

A protected disk labeled *miscellaneous files.*

Duplicate calendars that Camden already had sworn up and down to Wikström that he'd never seen.

Names that didn't match the Star Realm's population database or sound like local Therus ones.

A list of locations halfway across the planet.

All of it together had seemed likely enough that day in the Camden house in the woods, and had he been younger and more convinced the Star Realm needed the protection Shadow Force provided, he might have clung to the evidence. But now? Now it seemed . . . well, could it be too convenient?

There didn't seem to be anyone who wanted Camden in this much trouble, though. His wife and stepdaughters seemed to love him. At the very least, they likely enjoyed the money and status his position gave them. Camden's region tolerated him as much as they tolerated anyone employed by the Star Realm—but when it came right down to it, Cerethians knew if they didn't endure one of their own people ruling in the Star Realm's stead, they'd have a Vilarian in charge of things, and that was something they'd never risk. No, it was unlikely someone had implicated him for political purposes.

Which either meant he was guilty or had angered someone personally.

Kresten scribbled a few nonsensical words in the air with his finger. Camden didn't have many friends. An assistant, yes, but he had been adamant about work being the extent of his loyalty. No neighbors, not in the house in the mountains. His former neighbors in Cipra had all assured Wikström and Granqvist that *yes, sir, Camden was a fine man to have around. Always quiet, and those children of his were well-behaved. We missed him after he moved up the mountains.* There was his other daughter, but it'd only taken one message for Kresten to believe she had nothing against her father. As much as Rose Camden hated her sister, she loved him.

So.

Guilty?

It only made sense.

Berglund wouldn't be back for hours, so after a brief glance out the door, Kresten propped his feet up on the almost-empty desk and folded his arms. Nothing else had turned up from the searches of Camden's house and office. Not even the small microphone inside the mattress in his cell had provided anything of use—of course it would be too easy for the man to talk in his sleep.

He needed to go back to Cipra. Needed to search Camden's office once more, needed to visit his house again. He was missing something, and until he figured it out, he was stuck on Cereth. Sure, the Star Realm might be itching to make an example out of a puppet governor, but—

But what?

But he'd promised Ryllis nothing would happen to her father if he was innocent. It might not be a promise he could follow through, but he had to try. He owed her that much, even if the man was a bastard who he personally would never miss if he spent the rest of his life in that cell down the hall. But Ryllis cared, and he couldn't fault her for still loving him and caring for what happened to him.

With a sigh, he pushed himself to his feet and stuck his head out the door. Instead of the empty corridor he'd been praying for, Granqvist was marching toward him, brushing something from his hands. Kresten frowned.

"Meeting went that well?" Granqvist asked.

"He seems to think we can work magic." Kresten scratched at his chin. It was a frequent misconception in the Fleet outside of Shadow Force. "Or something."

"If only. Though it would be closer if we weren't hemmed in by bureaucratic nonsense."

"Bureaucratic nonsense is the way of things. Even on Cereth." Kresten leaned against the wall. "How's Camden doing?"

Granqvist muttered a few updates, but Kresten ignored all, save the most important words. He didn't care that Camden had spent most of his time sleeping or had barely eaten. If they never fed the man again, Kresten would lose no sleep over it. But Ryllis would, so he squelched the uncharitable thought.

"But no confession."

Granqvist rolled his eyes. "In your dreams."

Of course. "Then let's go talk to him. No sense in letting him get too comfortable."

"I thought you'd say that." Granqvist handed him a shock stick.

Kresten thanked him for the foresight and stuck it in his holster, all too conscious of how he'd first met Ryllis dressed like this. It seemed an eternity ago, yet yesterday at the same time. He'd never imagined—before or after he'd fallen in love with her—that her father would be in the same position one day.

My father has lost his mind.

As they walked, he braced himself against the unease that would surely flood him once he entered the cell block. The disquiet did rush over him as Granqvist unlocked the heavy metal door anyway, a deluge of fear and anger and despair. Not all the emotion was from Camden, of course—with his limited empathy, he couldn't differentiate between subjects—but it was enough to remind him, for the second time in all of five minutes, why he'd decided against this life.

The selfishness of that decision hit him a moment later. He was privileged enough to make that decision. The rest of the telepaths in Shadow Force weren't. They either joined the Fleet voluntarily or were imprisoned on a distant asteroid with suppression chips—or executed. The Fleet didn't care how uncomfortable they were as long as they fulfilled their duty. Granqvist, however, didn't flinch as they entered, so maybe not every telepath struggled with the same heightened empathy he did. Or maybe Granqvist had simply learned to control his feelings, a skill which had always eluded Kresten.

Granqvist pulled the door of Camden's cell open, and Kresten, after a deep breath, swung the shock stick against the wall. Camden glared at them through the static field that remained in the door, then sprang to his feet.

"You bastards. Come to gloat some more, have you? You've made a big mistake here. You think you'll get away with this? It'll never happen. I know people, I'll—"

"You'll do nothing." Kresten holstered his stick and leaned against the doorframe. The casual gesture had always annoyed Ryllis when she'd been in her father's position, and surely they weren't that different, underneath it all.

Camden spouted off a long storm of curses, most aimed at him, some aimed at Granqvist, a few aimed at both their mothers. Granqvist snorted, but Kresten narrowed his eyes. How could Ryllis possibly be upset that this man was out of her life?

"This could go a lot more amicably if you'd stop," he said. "Now, if you made a mistake, we can talk about this, maybe discuss what leniency can be had. Maybe someone threatened or blackmailed you. Maybe you didn't realize you were in too deep until it was too late, or maybe you've got some sort of good excuse. Let's talk about it—but civilly," he emphasized.

"Civil?" Camden's cheeks flamed as he threw his hands in the air and waved them around his cell. "You're going to call this civil? Nothing about this situation is civil, you pompous, spoiled, excuse of a man. You yank me from my family, my home, my job, and accuse me of treason, and you want to imply that there's any kind of respect on your side? You've been screwing with me since you arrived on Cereth, what with throwing your marriage in my face, and I won't stand for it."

His soul hurt, even though Ryllis would never hear those words. "I'll ignore that," Kresten replied, "if only out of respect for the service you've so dutifully provided the Star Realm for many solar cycles. Or has it been so dutiful?"

Camden's rage turned to a smirk. "Wouldn't you like to know?" He spoke rhythmically, almost a song.

Kresten wanted to reach through the field and grab him by the neck. That would have been possible in a few of the prisons on Vilaria where the fields were keyed to the genetic codes of the guards and interrogators, but not here on Cereth, where prisoners were only temporarily held before being released or transferred to the Eradication Council. *Too bad*. On the other hand, strangling Camden wasn't part of the plan, so maybe being forced to keep his hands to himself was for the best.

"You think you're so smart, don't you?" Granqvist growled. "You think you can hide anything from us? Even as a Cerethian, you're wrapped up so deep in Star Realm politics that I know you're smarter than that. Do you know what I can do to you?" A curt nod at Kresten. "What he can do to you?"

"I'd like to see you try it, child." Camden's sneer hadn't faltered.

Granqvist lunged at the field, and Kresten pulled him back, half unwillingly. Strangling Camden by proxy was a little more appealing than doing it himself. Even so, he didn't feel like cleaning anyone's blood up—or seeing it.

"Better be careful what you ask for, Camden," he said. To Granqvist, he added, "Let's go. Let him think about his future some more. Maybe we can check the schedule and let him witness an interrogation before he's subjected to it himself. Give him a second chance to be cooperative, you know?"

Granqvist grumbled a few Vilarian curses under his breath. Kresten would have laughed—it meant Granqvist saw him as a peer and not a prince—but he choked it down and put on his professional face. Later. He'd let himself laugh later.

"That's all you can do?" Camden hollered. "Swear at me, and not even to my face? It's a wonder you managed to conquer your manhood, much less a few planets."

Realm's sake, was he trying to get himself killed before he could confess to anything?

"Do you ever shut up?" Kresten asked him, slamming the door shut before Camden could answer. "That is not normal," he said to Granqvist, a little calmer.

"Over twenty solar rotations he's served us. I don't believe it. Who could put up with him for that long?"

Kresten chuckled. There was humor in the situation, but only until Ryllis flitted into his mind. How long had she dealt with the bastard? How long had she tried to convince him and his new wife to love her? Zaella Camden clearly disliked her stepdaughter —had she poisoned her father against her as well? She wouldn't be the first stepmother to do so, and suddenly, as the memories of the dark fog he'd experienced drifted back into his mind, he wanted nothing to do with that house in the mountains. The laugh faded, and he rubbed his head.

"You all right?" Granqvist asked.

Kresten shot a momentary glance his way. "Of course. A bit tired, I suppose."

"You seem more than a bit tired." The other man shrugged. "You faded out there for a second."

"I did?" Realm's sake, were the headaches turning into something else? He hadn't used telepathy, hadn't even thought about it.

"Just thinking of how much I don't want to question Zaella Camden again."

"Don't take this the wrong way, Westermark, but you don't exactly have the reputation for squeamishness."

"Yeah. Maybe that's the problem." Kresten froze. "You ever wonder how your life would be different if you weren't stuck with Shadow Force?"

"No." Granqvist paused and frowned at him. "It's not an option, so why bother wondering? Second-guessing things like that is a waste of time."

"I suppose you're right." Something unpleasant twisted in his gut.

"So. Zaella Camden."

"Yeah."

"It's you or me. Take your pick."

"I'll do it." The foul sensation grew. "I have an idea."

There was one thing that would throw Zaella off, and that was if he visited as His Imperial Highness—with his wife by his side.

here was no worrying about the bobcats this time. Bry had brought Ryllis's father's car to the shuttle site outside Cipra and waited, quiet and pale, though her reticence suited Ryllis. It wasn't as though her stepsister had ever apologized for the things she'd done and not done in the past, and until that happened . . . well, it wasn't as though they'd become friends. What would they talk about? The past? How terribly Zaella had treated her and how Bry had never said a friendly word to her? The now? How she was living in luxury on Vilaria and Bry's stepfather had just been arrested by the Fleet? Nothing seemed appropriate.

The uncomfortable silence lasted until they came to the stand of aspens where she'd seen Zaella last week. Their yellow leaves were completely gone after that snowstorm, leaving the trees bare and skeletal-like in the late autumn sun. Ryllis squinted at the circle of trees as they approached. Aspens grew rather quickly, but not that quickly, and she couldn't remember ever seeing them before leaving Cereth. Her memories weren't as sharp as they had been when she'd first met Kresten, but they weren't nonexistent, either. And if anyone would remember the look and feel of the woods, she would.

"Bry," she began, forcing a cordial tone into her voice. "Are those natural? They look so strange. And I can't remember them being here. Did one of the neighbors plant them?"

Bry's head swiveled toward her, then she focused back on the road. "I don't know. Not all of us can spend our time wandering the woods."

It was a clear slap in the face, and incorrect. Yes, she'd spent most of her free time wandering the forest, if Bry counted a few minutes each day before sunset *free time*. Zaella had tasked her with too many chores for much else. And naturally, Bry must feel some resentment—those same chores Ryllis had once been responsible for must have fallen to her and Greta for the past few solar cycles. Even a governor couldn't afford paid help, and non-Vilarians weren't allowed slaves.

"You know I didn't 'wander the woods', Bry." Ryllis hid a sigh, vocally at least. In the corner of her mind, Kresten made a displeased noise. "Zaella wouldn't have been happy with me had I done that."

"She took care of you," Bry replied. "Just as it was expected of her. She treated you like a daughter."

Is she delusional? Kresten cut in. *That woman was horrid to you. You know, if you'd like, I could always find something to accuse her of.*

Ryllis *tsked* him silently. *That's not funny. You can't keep threatening to arrest people who are cruel to me. And Bry is just in denial, I think. I'd probably feel the same in her place.*

He grumbled telepathically, and she sent a wisp of affection into his mind.

I'll make it up to you later.

"I'm not having this argument," she went on to Bry. "Not here, not now."

"It's not an argument. But you were ungrateful for everything she did for you. You still are. I'm sorry if you can't see that."

Ryllis clasped her hands together. Gripping Kresten's would have felt better, but she couldn't blame him for sitting behind her, away from Bry, though she was surprised her stepsister had let a Vilarian prince out of her sight. Likely Bry had trouble seeing Kresten as such, for what kind of prince would have lowered himself to marrying Ryllis?

Don't think I didn't hear that. What did I say about thinking that little of yourself?

Ryllis mentally rolled her eyes. *I meant her. That's what she's probably thinking. Why else is she so relaxed around you? Don't you remember how terrified I was when I found out who you are?*

Perhaps it's my charm? It's not my fault you weren't as susceptible to it at first.

What little charm you're showing her right now couldn't fill a thimble. She tried to sound angry, but a mental laugh broke through. *By the Realm, Kresten, just stop eavesdropping for five minutes and let me have a conversation with her.*

If you really meant that, you'd shut me out.

She shook her head at his insistent flirtatiousness and turned back to Bry. "Zaella was horrid to me." Then, a little softer, "I don't blame you, though. You were a child. Even if you'd noticed, there was nothing you could have done about it. And even now, I don't expect you to speak against her. Just to understand the things I went through."

Bry was silent.

"I really am curious about the aspens, though," she went on.

"I don't know." Bry focused out the window, then rubbed her eyes. "Mother always said you did it. That you created them, with your evil gift, and that I was not to go near them or talk about them to anyone. She said it would bring trouble down upon us, even though they were all your doing."

"She said I—" Her hand fluttered in nervousness. "Zaella knew about me? About my powers?"

"After we heard about your marriage, she said she'd guessed a long time ago."

Give me a break. Zaella would have turned you in before she kept your secret, even to protect herself.

She brushed Kresten away. "You don't really believe that, Bry. She'd have turned me into the Fleet had she known what I was capable of. Anything to get rid of me."

Hey! Don't act like you came up with that argument all on your own. Give me credit for it, at least.

Ryllis hushed him in her mind. Bry glanced at her, then back toward the trail.

"Having someone with the power to grow plants is useful on Cereth, you know," Bry said.

Bry wasn't wrong. There was always a need for more food in this area of Therus, if not more beauty. The Vilarians might take the first away as punishment when they felt like it, but they couldn't take the second, not without destroying their own lands. Still, for Zaella to have known about something like this and still kept it a secret was hard to believe.

"Maybe that's so," she said. "But in that case, turn us around. I want to see the aspens, close up. Maybe they'll remind me."

"Ryl—Your Highness—"

"Just do it, please," Kresten said from the back seat, verbal at last. *I'm not exactly looking forward to seeing Zaella again, either,* he added. *Any delay is good.*

Bry complied that time—no doubt the orders of a prince of the Star Realm carried more weight than her stepsister's—and by the time they stopped in front of the aspens, a little of Ryllis's anxiety had dissipated. Nature was nature, no matter how confusing and new, and it soothed every raw edge in her soul as soon as she stepped outside. Her shoes didn't crunch on much of anything this time—the rain and snow had turned the leaves and acorns into a slick mess. Bright yellow leaves filled the circle, and Ryllis picked one up and folded it between her fingers as she circled the small clearing.

"I don't remember this," she said to Kresten. "At all." *And it hasn't even been that long. What other parts of my old life will I forget before this is over?*

He stroked her mind. *You're the same person you always were.*

I suppose. She ran her hand down an aspen's trunk, trying to remember. The day before the Fleet had arrested her, she'd gone for a walk. It had been cold, and even the green scarf she'd worn hadn't been warm enough. Such a strange detail to recall when she couldn't even remember where she'd gone walking. Everything was so fuzzy, like clinging to a thread. *I feel like I never existed before, and I hate that.*

I wish I could— Kresten jerked his hand away from the fallen aspen leaves he'd been studying. *Do you feel that?*

Feel what?

I don't know. Like a sultry breeze. He looked around, bafflement in his expression. *Strange. I—*

Hot? Kresten, it's freezing. Are you getting sick?

He frowned at her, a look she hadn't seen in so long—not since the prison. "It's not freezing. And why you are speaking to me telepathically in front of someone else? Really, Ryllis, your manners are unbecoming of a member of the imperial family."

Her face grew hot that time. *Kresten—*

"What did I just say? Don't speak to me like that in front of Bryony. Use your voice."

She backed away, toward the car. Bry frowned at her, but that was nothing new. Anyone who'd just realized their company was speaking telepathically in front of them would do the same. And Kresten was right: it was rude. Still, they'd done it often enough. Not in front of family, except his brothers and sisters every so often, but . . .

Kresten made a huffing sound. "This is all a waste of time, anyway. Get back in the car, both of you. Zaella's waiting."

⁓

And Zaella was waiting—on the front porch, no less. Bry gave her a kiss on the cheek, and Ryllis followed Kresten up the stairs. If she could glare at his back, maybe some of her anger would dissipate. He was stressed and exhausted, surely, but that hadn't mattered before. He'd never treated her so poorly before. She sat a discreet distance away from him on Zaella's couch, and the worst thought of all hit her.

Maybe she was doomed to be unloved.

Her mother had loved her. Her father had too, at least until her mother had died and he'd thrown himself into his work. When Zaella had come around, he'd become even more distant and sharp, as though his new family was the only thing that mattered anymore.

And Kresten?

He'd married her, yes, but before he'd done that, he'd purchased her. Not with credits or crowns, of course, for that wasn't how the system worked in the Star Realm anymore, but he'd used his Eradication Council entitlement to *obtain* her. So what if he'd never had a slave before her? Perhaps he'd been saving those entitlements for the right person, and a governor's daughter, young and fairly attractive, would have cost him quite a few.

Kresten glanced toward her, the same hard expression on his face, and Ryllis checked the mental shields she'd thrown up. He didn't say anything in her mind, so they must still be in place. She missed the intimacy of his voice, but he'd made it clear that wasn't appreciated today. Fine. She wouldn't allow him to eavesdrop, either.

"I want to apologize for what happened the other day," he was saying to Zaella. "I know it must have come as a shock, and I'm committed to clearing him. I wish I could give you more of a timeframe, but these things can take time."

Zaella looked stunned at the apology. "I appreciate that, Your Highness. More than you know. It's been so hard . . ."

"I understand. And I'm doing everything I can to ease that difficulty as well."

Ryllis's head swiveled toward him. Zaella didn't deserve this kind of consideration. Even her father—not a half lunar cycle ago, Kresten had been furious with him for the way he'd treated her. The way he'd falsely accused her of treason and set this entire new life of hers in motion. Kresten wouldn't have forgiven either of them so soon.

"The taxes are due in less than a lunar cycle," Zaella said.

Ryllis's gut tightened. And with no income, she'd be unable to pay. It had never been a problem with the Camden family before, since a governor's salary covered more than enough, but the Star Realm taxed families of prisoners higher. And families of prisoners who had formerly brought in all the money . . . those had no chance. They usually ended up in prison as well most of the time, or in front of the Eradication Council.

Kresten sighed. "There will be no worries. I'll make sure that's taken care of as well."

Ryllis almost snapped his name, then stopped. It was imperial money he wanted to spend, and she had no say in it, even if she disagreed. It was becoming more and more difficult to not fantasize about Zaella herself standing in front of the Council.

"That will be acceptable, will it not, Ryllis?" he went on.

Her head snapped up. She hadn't been paying attention at all.

"I asked you a question. Paying your father's taxes will be acceptable to you?"

You asked me a question? she repeated. *Kresten, what's gotten into you?*

She spoke telepathically before she could stop herself, and Kresten's cheeks flushed. It didn't take a genius to figure out it was from anger.

"Just answer. Out loud, as I asked before."

His voice was firm. No, not just firm. Harsh. Ryllis stared at the tea Zaella had set in front of her, unsure if she could reach for it without her hands shaking.

"I don't have a problem with it," she said.

"Good. It's not your decision or your money, after all."

Her eyes widened. Kresten had never spoken to her like this, had never made an issue out of the disparities in their backgrounds.

"I never said—"

Had never said what? What was there to say? Why was she arguing with him? Hot tears formed, and before she could wipe them away—so this man who used to be her beloved husband didn't see—he narrowed his eyes.

"Stop crying," he snapped. "Really, I thought better of you. I wouldn't have brought you here if I'd known you were going to make a fool out of me."

Her heart sunk; her stomach lurched. This was wrong. Something was terribly wrong.

"Your Highness." Zaella pushed her tea to the side and looked at both of them with fresh interest. "Perhaps I could speak to Ryllis alone."

"Fine. See if you can make her stop crying, too."

Zaella was the last person she wanted to speak to, but the hostility Kresten was exuding made her ill. Ryllis didn't give him another look as she stood and followed Zaella into the kitchen. The fireplace was blazing, and she leaned against the wall next to it, trying to stop herself from shaking.

"The prince is acting rather strangely," Zaella said.

"Yes." Ryllis resisted sniffling, but just barely. "He is."

"Would you like to know why?"

Her chin jerked up. "There's a reason?"

"There's a reason." Zaella cocked her head, as though she wasn't quite ready to explain. "So, I'll ask you again—would you like to know?"

Ryllis nodded. Of course she wanted to know. Or did she? She was out of the reach of the Eradication Council now, but Kresten could still send her away if he tired of her. If he'd decided he'd made a mistake. She couldn't bear to think about a future without him.

"Fine, then." Zaella lifted a shoulder, almost indifferently. "He entered the aspen circle."

"Entered the aspen—" She shut her mouth. Something was gnawing at her gut. Something she was missing. "I—I don't understand."

"Naturally *you* wouldn't." Zaella sank into a chair and examined her. "It took me quite a while, you know."

"Took you a while . . ." Ryllis stared. "For what?"

"To figure out how to control the will of a telepath. When the prince first arrived, I could convince him you were all wrong for him, but only as long as he was within shouting distance. As soon as he retreated from me, my power over him vanished. Clearly, I needed to figure out something else. The aspen circle has held most of my power for the past few solar cycles, but he had to enter willingly for me to make the connection between his mind and my influence. You got him to do that for me, and I should thank you."

The truth hit her, sickening and raw.

"You're a sorceress." Ryllis wanted to back up, but there was nowhere to go except the roaring fireplace. "You've cursed him."

"Such old-fashioned terms." Zaella smiled. "Not that I'm surprised. It's what the Star Realm would call me, after all. I prefer to call myself a diviner."

"A diviner of evil."

A laugh. "That's right. Your father raised you to worship the Star Realm's Light. I don't blame him for that—it was the safe decision for a Star Realm governor, if shortsighted and limited. Once you were grown, I tried to convince him you were old enough to be indoctrinated, but he disagreed, and I didn't push things. It would have been too great a risk."

"And my father? Did you—divine him as well?"

"Him too, though not being a telepath, it took a few solar cycles and quite a bit of effort." Zaella sighed. "I had hoped you'd inherited your powers from him, but we haven't been lucky enough to find out if another child would be talented."

"You—" What Zaella wasn't saying was too much. "You married him in the hopes you'd have a gifted child?"

"No. Not then, at least. I didn't know you had an innate power until a few solar cycles after I came here. He was simply useful. Powerful, and wealthy as a Cerethian goes. And living out here in rural Therus was a brilliant way for me to protect my powers from discovery."

It was too much. Ryllis sank to her knees next to the fireplace, but the flames didn't touch the ice in her heart. "Why are you telling me this?" she asked.

"Oh, child." Zaella shrugged. "Why not? It's not as though you can stop me, and perhaps you might end up more useful to me if you knew the truth."

"Kresten could walk in here right now. I'd tell him. He would believe me." Maybe that was false bravado, but she needed to believe she was right.

Her stepmother chuckled. "Naïve girl. I've taken his mind. As of now he thinks you're a slave who tricked him into marrying you, and he wishes he could change the past. This very second, he's sitting on the couch hoping you never come back."

Kresten?

The only answer was silence. Had he blocked his mind to her? He rarely did so—perhaps when he was especially upset or anxious and didn't want her to feel the same. It had become a bit more frequent since they'd arrived on Cereth, but that wasn't a surprise either. Much of his Fleet work needed to be kept confidential.

Kresten, answer me!

"Keep that up and I'll break that bond, too." Zaella began to pace around the kitchen. "As of right now, I'm willing to let you walk away—but don't push me."

"But why?"

Zaella shrugged, catlike. "I'm not silly enough to think the Fleet will ever free your father. His Highness is a second-best option for a husband—or perhaps first."

"That's it?" Her voice had grown hoarse. "This is about marrying well?"

"Of course not. Not anymore. *Now* it's about learning what kind of gifted children I might have with him. With my power and his telepathy . . . well, Bry and Greta may have turned out to be disappointments, but I wouldn't have to be disillusioned by their lack of potential any longer. The imperial family has many genetic gifts—just think of the possibilities."

Ryllis shook her head. "But you can't."

"I'll make you a deal." Zaella pushed herself up from the chair and approached her. "Call it a challenge, if you must. I can tell you love him—let's see just how much."

CHAPTER ELEVEN

Kresten shifted on the sofa once more. The formerly soft silk cushion had become solid under his weight, like he'd been sitting here for much too long. The feminine voices that had filtered in from the kitchen for the past few minutes stopped, and the silence was shortly followed by the kitchen door slamming. A strange weight lifted off his shoulders, and he sifted through his memories to figure out the cause. What was he supposed to be relieved about? He couldn't remember. He couldn't even remember what he was doing here, and that was even more disconcerting.

"Her Highness has gone for a walk." Zaella slid next to him and poured him another cup of tea. "She said it's been a long day, and after the problems with her father, I think she needs a break from everything. I'm sure she'll be back soon, but you know how she loves to wander in the forest."

"Oh." A bit of that confusing, dark mist washed over him, and he blinked it away. "Ryllis went exploring? That's good."

It *was* good, wasn't it? Yes. It was. Ryllis had become more trouble than she was worth lately, what with her insistence on speaking to him telepathically and her concern about her father and her disloyal thoughts about his. What in the Realm had he been thinking when he'd stood there in front of the Eradication Council and asked for her? He'd used up all his entitlement credit with them, and now, even as a prince, he couldn't acquire another slave for almost an additional solar cycle. And he wanted more slaves, didn't he?

Of course he did.

"Now, about Tavis . . ." she went on.

Kresten blinked. What about Camden? Oh, yes. He was supposed to be investigating the regional governor of Therus. Ryllis's father. Shadow Force had him locked up back in Epuas, in fact. Everything else was a haze; remembering what had happened just yesterday was like wading through quicksand.

Oh, that was it. Camden had sworn and hollered at him and Granqvist. Today, Granqvist was questioning him once more, trying to wear him down, and he was here at the Camden house in the mountains to . . . to do what? He couldn't remember. He'd told Granqvist something before he'd headed up here. Was he supposed to search the house again? Question Ryllis's stepsisters about anything odd they might have seen?

No, that didn't sound right. Why hadn't he made notes? He'd never required them before, but Realm's sake, he was growing old and forgetful and was going to need to start.

Right. He'd come up here to make sure Zaella and her girls were taken care of. He'd pay their increase in taxes himself, no matter what Ryllis had to say about it, and then he would make sure they released Camden. Afterward, he'd have to work on making things right for Camden with the Star Realm, but that would be easy enough, wouldn't it?

A palm on his knee brought his attention back to the present.

"Captain Westermark?" Zaella was saying. "Your Highness?"

He blinked, suddenly back in his body. *Reassurance.* She was understandably anxious and frightened and needed reassurance that everything would be all right—and so he would give it to her.

"He'll be released," he said. "There's paperwork involved, and I'll have to convince the right people it's the correct thing to do, but I'll make it happen as soon as I can. I promise you he'll be freed and back in his position shortly."

"No, Your Highness. Don't do that. At least, there's something you need to know first." Zaella's eyes grew dark. Fear? Distress? He couldn't tell, and though he searched his memories for the training he'd apparently forgotten, nothing seemed familiar. "I didn't want to say as much in front of Ryllis, her and Tavis being so close, but I'm almost certain he's guilty of everything the Fleet has accused him of."

Well. That was an interesting turn of events. And suddenly, it made sense. He'd thought it himself, hadn't he? That if no one had a personal issue with Camden, he was likely guilty? And here was Camden's wife, nervously admitting her own husband could very well be a traitor.

"Has he said anything to you?" Kresten asked. "Confessed?"

"No. Nothing like that." She removed her hand from his knee and twisted the fabric of her skirt into a knot. "But he's been acting so strangely. Like he's hiding something. And I knew it was my duty to report any suspicion of disloyalty to the Star Realm and that I should have said something to the Fleet earlier, but—"

"But you love him. And turning him in was too difficult for you to even consider." Zaella nodded, and he sighed. Her loyalty and devotion to her husband, so unlike Ryllis's lukewarm allegiance, was impressive—and, he had to admit, alluring, like how the sunset spilled over a lake on a winter evening. "Right now, I haven't any reason to doubt you. Or suspect you of collaboration in whatever crimes he may have committed. That can always change, but I hope it won't."

How he hoped it wouldn't. Zaella didn't deserve what the Fleet would do to her.

"Please let me know what I can do to help," she said. "I wish things were different, and I still love him more than I want to admit—but I have to do the right thing in the eyes of the Star Realm."

"I understand that. And I appreciate your allegiance." He folded his arms and frowned. "A confession will be necessary, first of all."

"Does that seem likely?" Her eyes were wide, anxious, and he wanted to wrap his arms around her and tell her everything would be all right. "Tavis is so stubborn. I don't think he'll voluntarily admit to doing anything wrong, especially when he knows what's waiting for him afterward."

"Telepathically, yes, it'll be almost a sure thing." Kresten pushed himself to his feet and headed for the door. Zaella needed him, but the dark mist was back, and he hated the feeling of it washing through his veins. "I'll see what I can do to push through his interrogation. We'll know something soon. Until then, keep the faith."

"Please," she said. "Do it soon."

"I will." It surprised him how much he meant it. "I promise."

Granqvist, however, had different ideas when Kresten returned to the detention center in Epuas. Looked at him like he'd lost his mind, in fact.

"You know that's not policy." He furrowed his brow and regarded Kresten with confusion as they sat in the empty office with Camden's giant calendar still on the wall. "We're nowhere near that stage."

"Maybe not." By the stars, it was nice to not be trailed by that dark mist he'd been feeling lately. His mind was clear, and he needed that. "But there are exceptions to the policy. Camden's no ordinary rebel."

"No—oo. He's not." Granqvist's frown grew deeper, and Kresten wondered if he knew how much older the crease between his eyes made him look. "But I don't know why you're so eager to subject yourself to that kind of discomfort so quickly, Westermark. Berglund said you've struggled with headaches and fainting, and though I'd be perfectly willing to do it instead, he also said His Majesty was clear that you are to perform any telepathic interrogation when it comes to Camden. Apparently, he doesn't trust the rest of us."

"Berglund doesn't know a thing." Kresten waved him off and headed to the side table for another cup of coffee. No one, especially Granqvist, needed to know that the colonel's assessment of the situation was entirely too accurate. "I was overworked and tired, like I keep telling you. I'm sure everything will be just fine this time around."

Or I'll hit my head on the floor and never wake up . . .

"Do you plan on filing the exception request yourself? It has to, uh, come from the interviewing officer."

What a reminder. On the other hand, focusing on the paperwork was healthier—it certainly wouldn't do to keep focusing on his first telepathic interrogation since he'd resigned. Whether his blackouts were only from fatigue or something else, he didn't relish having another one, but he would never admit that to Granqvist. *There's nothing wrong with me* was his official stance from now on. Zaella needed his support, and she wouldn't get it if this charade dragged on and on.

"Then I'll file the request," he said. "Right after we're done here."

"It'll have to be sent to Vilaria for approval."

"Do you think I don't know that?" Kresten snapped.

Granqvist was right, and he hated him for it. It would be another two lunar cycles before approval arrived, if he was lucky. By that time Camden would have either confessed or the Fleet would have authorized him to use telepathy, anyway.

Screw bureaucracy. Zaella said to get it done.

"Just a reminder." Granqvist shrugged. "But if you have nothing else on your calendar at the moment, he's about due for another session." He gestured toward the detention area with his head. "You can file that paperwork afterward. Who knows? Maybe you won't need to."

Suddenly, all Kresten wanted to do was sleep, but he nodded. "Yeah. Sure. You lead, I'll observe?"

Granqvist nodded easy acquiescence, and Kresten grabbed a stun stick and followed him down the row of cells once more. This wouldn't be like last time. Camden wouldn't get the upper hand today, and Kresten wouldn't allow himself to be angered by anything the man said. Neither would Granqvist, if he had anything to say about it—but Realm's sake, Camden was truly obnoxious, and he wouldn't be able to blame Granqvist for slugging him. How had Zaella put up with him?

He thought about her smile and dark hair all the way to Camden's cell. Distractions could get one killed, but as distractions went, this one was almost undeniable. What was it about her? She wasn't attractive in any kind of conventional way, but she was striking in her own right, like a star in the wrong place at the right time. Did that even make sense, or had she somehow gotten in his mind that badly? That wasn't like him—even Elise hadn't turned his eye for several solar cycles after they'd met—but perhaps he'd simply never run across a woman like Zaella before.

Granqvist punched in the code to unlock the cell door, and Kresten forced the visions of Zaella from his mind, then steadied his feet. They were going to have to drag Camden out this time, and he didn't relish a fight, or even a muted confrontation.

From the bed, Camden glared at them as the static field shimmered. "Have you two come to ask some more inane questions?"

Granqvist, to Kresten's relief, didn't take the bait that time. "We just came by to have a little chat somewhere away from your cell. Surely you're ready for a change of scenery by now?"

Camden stood, all too easily, and Kresten's hand tightened on the stun stick. Something was up, and he'd be ready for it when it happened.

"Good," he said. "Turn around and face the back wall, hands on your head." Camden, to his surprise, complied with no argument, so Kresten nodded at Granqvist and keyed in the code to drop the field. He didn't trust Camden, especially after the things Zaella had said, but sometimes one just needed to take things at face value. Everyone tired of fighting, eventually.

Most everyone.

To Kresten's surprise, Camden didn't fight as they led him down the hall. He couldn't have known his wife had betrayed him, but he was certainly acting as if he did. The fight had simply gone out of him. He didn't even say anything as Granqvist shoved him inside the interview room, didn't move as Kresten restrained his hands in the manacle bar, then took his favorite spot against the wall. Could it be possible this was it? The anticipation of not having to use telepathy bathed him in hope.

"You're rather cooperative today," Granqvist began. His sneer had vanished—temporarily—and Kresten was grateful for that. As irritating as Camden probably found it, it wore on him as well. "Why?"

Camden gave a shrug that should have been accompanied by arm-crossing. Maybe not so cooperative, then. "Maybe I wanted to go for a walk."

"You knew where your walk would end up," Kresten said. "And yet you came with us, anyway. With little resistance, I might add. It's obvious you want to talk, and I can't blame you for that. So, let's do it. You'll feel better once it's all over."

It happened more frequently than most would ever suspect. Guilty consciences ate at some. Not all, but some. Camden didn't seem like he had any conscience left, especially after working directly for the Star Realm for so long, but it was always a possibility. When he remained silent though, Kresten cursed his hopefulness.

Granqvist tapped on his chin with a finger. "This will go better for you if you do, Camden."

It was a predictable threat, but Camden's cheeks grew red with rage. "You think I'm stupid enough to believe that? You think there's a good way out of this for me? I've never seen a single person released once the Fleet has their claws in them, so you can take that pathetic, unoriginal script and shove it—"

"Come on now." Kresten pushed off the wall. "You know that's not true. Unless you're hiding something. Which I think you are."

Camden's jaw tensed.

"If that accusation bothers you," Granqvist added, "then prove to us you aren't."

"I—" His jaw didn't relax in the slightest, and his fingers clenched and released in a pattern that set Kresten's own teeth on edge. "I don't know. I don't think I can. I just don't know how."

"Fine." Granqvist folded his hands. "Talk to me about the calendar first."

"The—calendar?"

Camden was stuttering now, and that was why Granqvist was focusing on a series of questions that weren't all that important on their own while Kresten watched and analyzed and came up with their next move. By the Realm, but it would be easier to strap Camden down and read his mind. That was what Zaella would want him to do, and for some reason he couldn't quite identify, she was probably right. Did he dare tell Granqvist that Camden would never confess? Granqvist would doubtless ask how he knew that, and how would he ever explain what Zaella had said? *His wife thinks he's guilty* was useful, yes, but it only went so far, and just like Granqvist had reminded him, there was a procedure for these things.

The wall grew cold behind Kresten's back, and he shifted. Granqvist was staring at him oddly. So was Camden, come to think of it. Had he fallen asleep?

"Ignore Captain Westermark," Granqvist said. "The calendar. The one in your office at home. You know what I'm talking about."

Camden's shoulders sank, and Kresten eyed him carefully. Resignation? It would seem so, and with anyone else, he wouldn't have been surprised, but there was something off about the man. Yes, there it was in his expression, though he was trying desperately to cover it.

Defiance.

"Oh," Camden said. "I don't think I want to talk anymore. To either of you."

"You don't want to talk anymore?" Kresten asked, temporarily not caring that Granqvist was the one who was supposed to be asking questions. "Guess what? You don't get to make that decision."

Camden swore at him under his breath, words Kresten hadn't heard in a dozen solar cycles, and before Granqvist could stop him, he was off the wall, his hands around Camden's throat. Camden couldn't reach up to stop him, but he kicked wildly, pushing his chair to the floor and forcing himself to his feet. The motion knocked Kresten to the side, but he ground his boots into the floor and held firm. Camden's knees buckled, and Kresten squeezed harder, relishing the feel of skin under his palms. Why hadn't he done this before? Camden needed to be shown, he needed—

A great force shoved him, and his hands flew off Camden's neck as he tripped, unable to maintain his balance that time. Before he could say a word about the interruption, Granqvist had shoved him out the door and against the wall in the gray corridor. Kresten froze. Perhaps he'd gone too far.

"What in the Realm was that, Westermark?" Granqvist's cheeks were red with fury. "I don't know how you normally run things, but that wasn't part of the agreement, and you can't just go beating up on a prisoner, especially when he might lead us to an entire insurgent group!"

"That arrogant bastard thinks he has any say in what goes on here. He's no longer the governor of Therus, and he needed to be taught a lesson of just who's in charge—he required a reminder it's not him, and I gave it to him since no one else seemed inclined."

If Granqvist was offended, he didn't show it. "You could have killed him!" he all but hollered.

"So what? You're honestly going to say the Star Realm isn't better off without him?"

"We've already removed him from his position. Killing him isn't your decision." Granqvist shoved his hands in his pockets and paced in circles around the corridor. "I don't know what your problem is. When you showed up here, you were professional, calm. Now . . . Realm's sake. I can't imagine the stress you must be under, but you're making things worse."

When the chair had been knocked over, Camden had pushed him against the table, however accidentally, leaving a burgeoning bruise on his knee. By the stars, he'd regret this tomorrow, but he'd been desperate. Zaella had *said* what he needed to do, and Granqvist would never understand.

"I think I'm going to go file that paperwork," he said, his breath becoming normal. "Then none of this will matter."

"Yeah. You do that." Granqvist stalked off down the hallway, turning just once. "Because I'd hate to find out what His Imperial Majesty would do to either of us if you foul this one up."

CHAPTER TWELVE

*S*pending the night in the woods hadn't been ideal, but there hadn't been any other option. Zaella's house was out of the question, and the barn had been locked when Ryllis had tried to sneak into the loft the night before. Zaella's doing, no doubt. There was no way of knowing whether it had been intentional or simply a nightly routine, but her stepmother had to know how much she liked the place.

She'd been relieved to learn that the small cave where she'd spent so many evenings alone as a child still existed. Slightly more than an overhang, it kept her dry from the morning dew, and now that the snow from the earlier storm had melted, the sun through the bare trees was warm, even in late autumn. She'd sat inside the cave in a heap of leaves and watched Kresten's shuttle depart through the skeleton-like branches, back to Epuas, unsuccessfully fighting back tears that no one except the birds witnessed.

But it was so difficult to believe Kresten had turned on her. The things he'd said and thought about her—what if Zaella was wrong? What if this was just more cruelty on her part? She'd said other harsh and crushing things in the past, after all. And if this was all made up as some sort of torment . . . well, it was hard enough to accept that Kresten was under some sort of spell, but what if Zaella actually had convinced him to see her as nothing more than a manipulative slave? Had she told him lies, repeated the things she'd said to Bry and Greta when Ryllis had been a child? Would that be worse?

Shivering from an emotion she couldn't quite pinpoint, Ryllis unburied herself and hurried through the forest. The snow had melted, but small patches of icy mud remained, and the ground was slick under her feet.

Her brisk walk slowed, and she sank to her knees to let the power of the trees and wind and birds rush over her. It helped, for a moment, and as she ran her fingers through the cool forest soil, her thoughts cleared.

If Zaella had done something to Kresten, that meant he still loved her, deep down. It meant he needed her. And that meant there was no way to fix this except to do what Zaella had asked of her. To bring back what she needed.

Spring violets.

Goat wool, woven with silver.

A mouse's skull.

She tucked her feet underneath her and stroked a fallen leaf, still streaked green, as she thought. Violets were nonexistent in this part of Therus during this part of the solar cycle, but clearly Zaella had already known of her gift, knew she could coax both plants to life. Bringing a dormant plant back to life had always been risky, and not something she liked to do—a certain empress's extinct flower notwithstanding—but out here in the forest, no one would take notice of a single flowering plant. And it was legal for her now, as long as she remained a member of the imperial family. Easy enough.

And how long will you remain so?

She brushed the thought away. There was no sense dwelling on what Kresten might or might not do.

The skull—such a horrid thing for Zaella to demand of her. Well, death like Zaella revered begat more death. That piece of the puzzle shouldn't be a surprise, but she wouldn't think of it further. To do so would flirt with a darkness that she couldn't bear to acknowledge, let alone take part in.

But the goat wool? Whatever Zaella had wanted that for, it seemed an impossible task—which was likely the point.

But first things first.

Violets, flowering or not, didn't grow at this elevation. She'd have to hike lower, and if the weather didn't hold out, it was dangerous to stray too far from her sheltering cave. Scouring her memory, she recalled a meadow a few kilometers below her, and even though the plants wouldn't be blooming, she could handle the walk and the violets. Zaella hadn't said they needed to look pretty, just be flowers.

It grew warmer as she descended the mountain on an old bobcat trail, narrow and muddy though it was. The morning was bright, and as she avoided the largest of the puddles, the peace of the woods absorbed into her soul. This was her home, no matter what the Star Realm said about her father, or how long she'd been gone, or how much she loved Kresten and couldn't imagine life without him.

A shadow crossed the trail, and she froze. It didn't feel like an animal, not exactly, but there was something . . .

Maybe her senses had dulled from so much time on Vilaria? Likely they had. She felt the deer and rabbits on Kresten's mountain now, though when she'd first arrived, they'd been nothing but a vague sense of nature. This was different. Unfamiliar, yet comfortable, like she'd forgotten, but somewhere deep inside, she hadn't. She peered through the branches that danced in the wind, but they only made the shadows more complex. Something beckoned her though, and she took a few small steps forward.

"Is someone there?" she called. Limbs creaked in the breeze. "Hello?"

She screeched in surprise as a mouse skittered across her shoe.

A mouse skull. Dare she? Could she even catch the creature? Sinking to her hands and knees, she searched the undergrowth for wherever it had disappeared to. A rust-colored mouse would be difficult to find in the autumn leaves, but it was better than trying to stumble across another one.

You had better not. I like my head just where it is, thank you very much.

Ryllis sprang to her feet.

"Who is that?" she asked, spinning in circles. It didn't sound like Kresten, but Kresten was the only one who spoke into her mind like this. Though it wasn't feminine either, which ruled out Zaella. Not that it was masculine. It was—

Down here, human.

Ryllis glanced down. Her rodent quarry sat under a withered mayapple, looking up at her, with what she could have sworn was a smug expression. The command hadn't exactly been polite, either.

You look surprised, it went on. *It's like you've never had anyone speak in your brain before—which I suspect you have, by the way you're staring at me.*

"A mouse?" Had Zaella done something to her mind? "You're talking to me? But that's not—"

You can speak to nature, can you not?

"How did you know that?"

Well, you looked down when I told you to. I try to catch the attention of every human who comes through these parts, and you're the first to acknowledge my presence in any kind of intelligent manner. Or perhaps not so intelligent, it added after a beat. *But close enough.*

Animals don't speak to me. Thanks to Kresten, the switch to mental speech was faultless as she crouched down in front of the mouse. *They simply—I feel them. I can understand them, most of the time. They don't speak to me as humans speak to each other.*

Are you not speaking to me right now, human?

Literal, bad-mannered rodent.

Well, yes, but I—

Good. It stood upright and flicked its tail. *I need your help.*

She gritted her teeth. *I don't have time to help you.*

You ought to make time, Ryllis Camden. It was your stepmother who did this to me.

Ryllis fell backward, eyes wide. *How do you know my name?*

We've lived near each other since you moved to Cipra.

Her mouth moved silently. *But that was—*

Years ago, yes. The mouse focused on her. *And yes, I am still alive.*

Realm's sake. Kresten's choice of words flew into her mind before she could stop them. *You're not actually a mouse.*

And you're not actually Vilarian either, but you can certainly sound like one when you want to, can't you? Is it such a surprise I might not actually be a mouse?

Picking up a phrase is a much different matter than—

Not, it replied with another flick of its tail, *where Zaella Camden is involved.*

Ryllis sat back on her heels and rubbed her eyes. The breeze picked up, and she stared at the mouse. Did she have an obligation to help it? As Zaella's stepdaughter, as whoever she was in the Star Realm now?

I didn't know she was capable of such things. She held out her hand, and the mouse jumped into her palm. *And I certainly don't know how to fix it.*

She does. The mouse looked up at her and hesitated. *Though how to convince her to spill her secrets . . . I do not know.*

Then what can I do for you until then?

Get me out of these woods? Surely you must have a comfortable place for me to sleep.

I— What would Kresten say if she brought a mouse back to the villa? Could this creature speak to *him* as well? His telepathy was limited to his spouse and his subjects—who required an entire process to speak to—but then again, she'd never expected to meet a talking mouse, either. *Like where?*

Even between two walls would be better than constantly dodging predators.

I may not be able to change you back.

It stared at her. *I know,* it finally said.

Do you have a name? A stupid question. It'd had a name at some point in its life.

She could have sworn the mouse smiled.

Violets.

She found a small clump under a maple tree, brown and half frozen. With Alder curled up asleep in her pocket, she dropped to her knees, brushed off the fallen leaves off the flowers, and breathed a few slow breaths on top. The gesture felt silly, since it was her presence, not her breath, that would restore them, but she couldn't get Kresten's strange actions and comments off her mind. Anything to speed his release would be welcome, silly or not. The mouse in her pocket didn't help her frame of mind, either.

The clump of violets grew warm under her palm. Almost afraid to look, she lifted it and found a few buds. Not quite enough. She stroked the larger of the two with a gentle finger, and it responded immediately, opening into a brilliant bloom more suitable for spring than the end of autumn. She hated to pluck it, but it would stay just as alive in her pocket, even dispatched from its usual source of life.

It was enough to remind her of the yellow flower Kresten had once left under the mattress in her prison cell. He'd cared about her, even when they were nothing more than enemies. He'd wanted her to smile, even in a place where smiles were forbidden and joy didn't exist. Had he left the flower for her or himself? Maybe it didn't matter—he'd seen something in her, even back then, and that wasn't something to discount. How could he have changed that quickly?

Alder?

You're ruining my nap with all this walking and magic and talking. What do you want?

Were you—Realm's sake, this was going to sound rude. *Were you married? When you were—when you were human?*

The mouse scoffed in her mind. *I'm still human. I simply don't look it.*

She stuck out a finger and gave him a quick stroke on the head. *I see.*

That feels nice. And to answer your question, no. Women are more trouble than they're worth. So is romance. Why, years ago, when I first met Zaella, she was the loveliest—

Yes, fine. I don't care to hear how lovely you thought she was. Forget I asked. And you can forget more pats on the head, too.

Do you hold grudges like this with everyone?

Ryllis settled on the ground and stared at the violets, incongruent with the melting snow.

No.

You don't sound certain.

What, you're some sort of emotional doctor now?

I can feel your emotions. Alder scampered into her hand and looked up at her. *And they're very distracting.*

I don't know what they'd be distracting you from. You're a mouse.

That was cruel.

She sighed and gazed out into the trees. Most of the snow that had clung to the leaves was gone now, and beads of water dripped from their bare limbs.

It was, and I'm sorry. I'm simply—I don't know how to fix this.

This being?

Zaella—she didn't just change you. She did something to my husband as well, and I don't know how to fix it.

Alder was silent for a long while. *Then you don't have any idea how to fix me, either.*

No.

"Your Highness?" A low curse. "What are you doing?"

Ryllis sprang to her feet at the Vilarian voice behind her. Wikström was picking his way through the thick underbrush that had practically parted for her, a displeased expression on his face. Well, of course. She hadn't returned to the villa with Kresten, and someone would've been out looking for her. She wouldn't ask what excuse Kresten had given for her non-arrival, just like she wouldn't ask how Wikström had found her.

"I went for a walk. Yesterday." She shoved the flower in her pocket, ignoring Alder's grunt. *Don't eat that, you ornery thing.* "I suppose I went a bit too far, and I got lost, but I didn't think— everything's fine. These are my woods."

He eyed her then, his eyes narrowed into slits, and she remembered for the first time since they'd met that he was

Shadow Force. But that didn't matter any longer. It wasn't as though he was going to pin her down and read her mind, not in the middle of the forest.

But perhaps when we get back to the villa . . .

"A bit far? That's an exaggeration, I believe. But if you're well . . ." His frown didn't abate. "Captain Westermark is back in Epuas. Urgent business, I'm afraid." If he knew the truth about why she was out in these woods—or that she'd just shoved Alder back into her pocket—it was impossible to know. "I'm to collect you and bring you back as well."

Ryllis pushed herself to her feet, giving Alder a light stroke. She'd have to get away from Wikström somehow, but darting through the woods didn't have the same appeal it used to. Besides, the lieutenant would know something was wrong if she bolted. Best to—best to what?

She had to stay. Being in Epuas with Kresten was unthinkable with the hold Zaella had on his mind. And goat wool and a mouse skull? The violets she had, yes, but how could she get them to Zaella without Wikström and the rest of the security personnel following her all the way back here?

"I'd much rather stay here." She steeled her tone, matching the one Kresten used occasionally. "Perhaps I can find a lodge in town for some time to myself. I'm sure you can understand that."

Like he'll believe a princess needs a holiday from her holiday.

Shut up, Alder.

Wikström shifted. "I—Your Highness, it's really not my decision."

"No. It's mine. Isn't it?"

You tell him.

Ryllis made a hushing noise in her mind, and Alder went silent.

Wikström sighed, hands on his hips. "You don't want to put me in this position, ma'am."

"Why not? Because you don't want to be seen dragging me

back to Epuas?" She steadied herself. What Shadow Force was capable of—what they'd already done to her—was never far from her mind.

"I'm not going to drag you back, ma'am. Just—" He sighed again and looked off into the distance. "Just tell me why you really walked away from the Camden house."

For the briefest of moments, she considered it. But Wikström would never understand. No Vilarian would, really. And even if he could understand it, he'd never *believe* it, and that was what she needed: someone to believe her. That Kresten's mind was being controlled, that she had a talking mouse—who used to be a man—in her pocket, and that the only hope for both of them were out-of-season violets, a mouse skull, and—

Silver goat wool.

Zaella's command echoed in her mind. Best to find the silver goat wool and a mouse's skull while she still could. While Kresten—and maybe even Alder—still had a chance. Before she lost her nerve and succumbed to Zaella's campaign of fear—a fear which, Ryllis suddenly realized, had been started long before now.

"I told you," she said over her shoulders, walking south toward the road where Wikström had doubtless come from without waiting for him to follow. "I just needed a walk. But I'm ready to go back to Epuas now."

Wikström hollered something back, but she ignored him as she tromped through the damp leaves. Maybe it didn't matter if he believed her or not. Maybe she could still use him to find the things Zaella wanted.

And she knew just the place to look.

CHAPTER THIRTEEN

ikström had been silent as they'd headed back into Cipra, he'd stared at the window on the shuttle that took them to Epuas, and now, as the autopilot sped through the streets, taking them back to the villa, Ryllis could practically feel him thinking. About what, she wasn't sure. There was no way Kresten could hide his current disdain for her, and Wikström was no doubt wondering what she'd done to deserve such treatment. It was awkward and humiliating and distressing, all wrapped up in one package that sickened her soul.

You really must stop these constant lamentations. Alder shifted in her pocket, awake at last. *It's distressing to everyone else around you, especially those of us who can hear your thoughts.*

She flinched, then ran a hand through her hair to cover her surprise. *Correct. My thoughts. And you really must stop jumping into them like that. Anyway, I hardly think Lieutenant Wikström is distressed at my . . . lamentations.*

I wasn't speaking of the Vilarian. He can break down in tears for all I care.

Tears? Ryllis suppressed a snort, and Wikström's head jerked up at the sound. She coughed once, a poor cover of her mistake, then waved him away. *Highly unlikely Lieutenant Wikström will fall for that. I doubt he even knows how to cry.*

How sad. Though I suppose not everyone can have a soul. The mouse turned in a circle, then settled down once more. *How much longer? I'm hungry. And stiff*, he added.

Not too long, I should think. Only another few minutes, but then I'll have to sneak you out of my pocket and stash you somewhere with no one seeing. What—what do you eat, anyway?

Hmm. Olives would be nice. I've never had one, but I hear they grow where we're going. Seeds, maybe. Cracked wheat. Raspberries. He paused. *Other mice, if that's all I have.*

Other mice? That's what you've been eating? She put her hand to her mouth. *I think we can do better than other mice—there are plenty of olives. Realm's sake, if you can climb a tree, you can eat them just like that.*

That's good. Because the more I think about, the more those olives are truly sounding—

"I wonder"—Wikström turned to her, unintentionally interrupting Alder's rant—"how a man who was deliriously in love with his wife just a few days ago could have changed his mind so quickly. It's like something flipped inside of him, and it's a very uncomfortable thing to be in the middle of. Not trying to sound unprofessional, but I'd be lying if I said it wasn't concerning."

Ryllis's head whipped around as she shoved Alder deeper into her pocket.

"I don't know what you're talking about," she replied. "Though I would say it's very much inconsiderate to speculate on the status of your superior's marriage."

Wikström didn't flinch at her reprimand.

"Don't deny it, Your Highness. He sent a message earlier today, and it went something like this: *My wife is on a long hike through the woods—some Cereth thing. Make sure she doesn't hurt herself, I suppose. It would look bad if something were to happen to her.*" He shrugged. "It was strange. And so very unlike the man who first arrived here, the one who was worried sick about your safety and happiness. Something has happened, and unlike what he's implied, I don't believe it has anything to do with you."

What was she supposed to say? The truth about what Zaella had done to Kresten? How would she prove it if she wanted to? Even if she let Alder out, let Wikström see him, it wouldn't matter, since they wouldn't be able to communicate. Besides, Wikström would never believe the truth, and why should he? Innate powers were one thing—brainwashing a Shadow Force telepath was something completely different.

"He is Vilarian, married to me or not, and he feels anything Cerethian is beneath him," she replied, surreptitiously stroking a finger across Alder's back to calm herself. "I doubt he'll ever understand our fondness for rambles through the woods, and frankly, I like it that way. It allows me to cling to at least a part of the life I once had."

She folded her arms and stared out the window. There. That would have to do. Because even if Wikström believed the truth, who knew how he would react? He was a liability now that the wrong person could control him. Emperor's son or not, he was only protected so far. They'd both learned that last solar cycle.

"I want to help," he said in response to her silence. "I know this isn't a marital spat."

The Vilarian knows nothing. Don't fall for his trickery.

"You're Vilarian." Ignoring Alder's commentary, as similar as it was to her own, she looked out the window. "Why would you help me?"

"You're Vilarian now, too, Your Highness. If my duty is to the Star Realm, that includes you as well. It certainly includes Westermark."

Ryllis scoffed.

Vilarian.

Hardly.

Now you're talking, came the voice from her pocket. *Don't let him fool you with that fake sympathy and concern. He doesn't see you as anything but a backwoods, second-rate choice of a wife from a conquered planet.*

Thanks, Alder. That's definitely—reassuring. Or something.

"You can make that sound all you want, ma'am, but Cereth is your past."

"And we're all tied to our past, are we not, Lieutenant? We're both standing on the surface of it, after all."

He should know better. She'd left Cereth, had thought she'd never return, and here she was—a stranger on her own planet, unable to move forward because of her father's choices and her own identity.

"More than you know, I suppose, since you aren't aware of my past—or my future." His gaze became . . . peculiar, if she had to pick a word. Heavy. Uncomfortable. "I'm not just a telepath, you know."

Her heart skipped a beat. That was what the heavy feeling was —the Shadow Force-like stare of his that made her skin crawl. For a moment, he'd looked so human—well, of course he was human, but so much like an *ordinary* human—that she'd forgotten he was a telepath to begin with.

And if he was anything like Kresten, he had heightened empathy as well, a side effect of his telepathic innate gift. He could feel her emotions if they were strong, and they had been all the way back from the mountains. As annoyed as Alder was with her ruminations and internal sulking, Wikström was likely doubly so. Maybe she was lucky he *hadn't* started crying at the dark feeling that filled the car and seeped into his psyche.

She lifted her chin in absurd defiance. Not that she cared what either of them thought of her.

"No? I thought most endowed Vilarians only had one innate gift." She forced casualness into her tone as the olive trees became more and more dense outside the window. If nothing else, they were almost back to the villa, where she could hide from his prying questions. "What else are you capable of?"

He gave her a flat smile. "I can visualize people's motivations without reading their minds. Hardly useful to the Fleet, if we're being honest, since you can intend to do something, then decide against it. It's a little more valuable in retrospect, and I've honed that ability since joining Shadow Force."

It didn't seem like a threatening power, though of course the Star Realm didn't care about that. Shadow Force would have impressed Wikström into service just like everyone else who didn't want to be implanted with a suppression chip and then imprisoned.

"I—I don't understand," she replied. "How is it valuable? And what does it have to do with Kresten? Or me?"

Careful with this one, Alder interjected. *He seems to know something, and it better not have anything to do with the fact I'm here.*

"Nothing, I suppose. Not directly, at least." Wikström frowned at her side, almost as if he'd noticed the mouse's presence. "It's Mrs. Camden. She fairly screams malevolent to me, enough that being in that house is more uncomfortable than even you can imagine, in a way Westermark's limited empathy can't touch. I don't know what she's doing there—or if she's done anything, in fact. It may simply be her personality. I've run into people who are simply unpleasant to be around, though at that point it takes getting to know them a bit to decide they're not a threat."

He stopped, as if he was waiting for her to say something. When she didn't, he went on.

"But Mrs. Camden projects a pleasant image on top of everything dark I feel underneath, so I doubt that's what I felt there. She's not simply a disagreeable person deep down, and that bothers me. I think you could solve the mystery, if you were so inclined. I think you know why I'm so uncomfortable in that house."

"Are you threatening me?" She meant it to come out as a warning of her own, but it sounded like a desperate plea instead.

"No." He frowned as if she'd asked the silliest question he'd heard in the long time. "Of course not. I know that whatever I'm feeling has nothing to do with you, even though I can feel that it's bothering you. I'm simply trying to figure out why that cottage is the most distasteful place I've visited in a long while."

Ryllis leaned back in her seat and considered him. How was she supposed to explain everything Zaella had told her, everything she had done to Kresten? Could she? Did she even want to? Or, if she did, would Wikström send the Fleet after Zaella, not caring that harming her could leave Kresten permanently under this spell?

"Zaella—" she began, then stopped. Once she said it, there was no going back. And maybe there was no hope for Kresten, anyway. "She did something to him. Changed him."

She'd planned on shocking him with her statement, but he simply nodded.

"I suspected as much. I don't know the man well, but he's been nothing short of erratic over the past half lunar cycle. Odd for his position—both of them." Wikström folded his arms and nodded at her once more to keep going. "Do you know what she did?"

"I think so. Some of it, anyway." He sounded accepting of the matter, helpful, almost, and her heart beat a little slower. "There have always been rumors in the mountains, for as long as we've lived there. Forever, really. And they aren't rumors, exactly— they're so old that they're more like myths. You Vilarians—especially the Fleet and Shadow Force—you think you ran out the old faiths hundreds of solar cycles ago, the ones who survive on evil, but there are still some who practice, even though they're forced to do so in secret. I didn't know Zaella was one of them until she told me just yesterday. She must have kept it quiet because of who my father was."

"He would have been quite the target for—what would you call it here on Cereth? An enchantment?"

Ryllis nodded. "And my father. She admitted she manipulated his mind, though it took a few solar cycles. It didn't work as quickly as it did with Kresten."

"Westermark's arrival brought out her true nature, and his telepathy made it easy for her to break into his mind."

"I think so."

And now, through Kresten's mind, Zaella would have access to Realm knew how much information, both imperial and Shadow Force. The sinking feeling grew—the Fleet would never allow him to live.

"Hmm." Wikström scratched his chin as the car slowed. "She told you this?"

"All of it." Ryllis sighed. Was that the truth? What other secrets did Zaella have? "Well, as far as I know."

Wikström crossed his leg over his knee and stretched his arm along the seat next to him. It was a casual move, but something told her it was anything but.

"But why?" he asked. "She has nothing to gain by informing you of her plans."

The car became oppressively hot, and Ryllis fanned a hand in front of herself. What would Wikström think about this part of her story? She didn't need to ask herself—she knew. Anyone who knew anything about the Vilarian Star Realm would know.

"She said she would—" Ryllis wound her fingers together in her lap. "She said she would free him from the spell if I gathered some things for her."

"What things?" His expression grew icy. "You can't possibly believe she would, even if you followed through."

"I don't know what else I can do. Do you think I could just waltz up to his commanding officer and say *someone enchanted my husband and I need your help*?" She bit her lip. "I have to try, if even to buy him some more time. If the Fleet finds out what she's done, they'll arrest her then quite possibly kill her, or do something else to her that will prevent her from releasing him. And when I think of what they might do to him if they find out his mind has been compromised—I can't risk that. I have to save him."

Wikström narrowed his eyes at her, reminding her that she had, in fact, just informed the Fleet.

"Well, you're probably right," he replied, his gaze sharp. "But maybe it can remain a secret for a little while longer. I doubt whatever she's done will become worse if we wait a day. What did she want from you?"

Ryllis pulled the little violet from her pocket. The one without Alder in it—even though she hadn't known he was starving when she'd placed it there, she hadn't trusted him not to eat it. It hadn't wilted a bit, its deep purple as vivid as that of a spring day, but Wikström already knew of her power, so that didn't matter.

"This. I suppose she knew no one else but me could find living flowers this time of the solar cycle. And then—" She ran her finger around the bloom. "Goat wool spun with silver. And a mouse skull."

"Oh, is that all?" His eyebrows sprang up. "For another spell, no doubt."

"Possibly. I know it sounds foolish, but what else could I do?"

"Your Highness, if you're right that she practices some ancient and evil mountain faith, you cannot give these to her." Wikström didn't appear at all amused by her attempt at levity. "You know I must report this. She cannot be allowed to continue this work, especially at the cost of the imperial family—and a telepath."

"I don't know what she plans to do with them. For all I know, she wants to make a little mouse decoration for her kitchen."

Guilt settled onto her shoulders. He wasn't wrong, but she managed a half-smile. Kresten deserved more than his fate under Zaella's control—and if Zaella was dead, he would never be the same person again. His life might be forfeit as well, for prince or not, the Fleet couldn't risk a telepath who could be controlled by someone else. And his father, though saddened, would be duty-bound enough to order his death over it.

"If you make this official," she went on, "I doubt he will ever be free. I promise you that, not that I have to remind you what'll happen if I can't fix this. I have to help him and just need a bit of time to figure out how I might do that. But until then, I need to act as though I'm following through on her demands."

At that, it was Wikström's turn to look out the window. Except for the noise of the cobblestones underneath, the transport fell silent as it slowed in front of the villa. She might not be a telepath, but it wasn't difficult to read his mind as he sat there, even as the door opened.

Is my loyalty to the Fleet or His Highness?

"I will do what I can," he said after a moment. "However little that might be." Ryllis drew in a breath, and he held up his hand. "On one condition—no matter what, you do not allow her to use the items for evil."

It was a start, but he assumed she had much more control over Zaella than was possible.

"How do you propose I do that?" she asked.

"That's up to you, Your Highness." Wikström's lip curled in a half smile. "This goat wool, though—where do you plan on getting it?"

Ryllis left Alder in the villa's garden for his long-awaited feast of olives, and Lavinia nudged her hand in greeting as she entered Alessia's backyard, the little girl on her heels. She stroked between the goat's horns, marveling at the difference in the animal. Her coat was silky, almost shiny, and her eyes were bright, a marked improvement from when Ryllis had first met her.

"But I don't understand." Eyebrows drawn together, Alessia glanced from Ryllis to the goat. "Surely you didn't need to come here for some goat wool."

"You have some, don't you?"

"Yes, but—why her?"

Wikström cleared his throat, and Ryllis shot him a look.

"Alessia, no one can know we were here, do you understand?" Ryllis asked. "No one can know what we wanted with Lavinia. It's important. And I'll pay you well for the wool."

"Pay me?" Her lips pursed. "The Star Realm doesn't pay for anything. They take what they want, and then they leave."

"But I'm Cerethian first, right?" Against her will, Ryllis smiled, then pulled two gold crowns from her pocket and handed them over. "These are yours. Not your mother's. Do you understand that?"

Alessia's eyes widened as she stared at the coins in her palm. No doubt it was the most money she'd ever seen—or even imagined. "We just sold the last bit of yarn yesterday. But I can spin more if you have a few minutes."

"You need the silver spun in with it, anyway," Wikström interrupted. "In case you'd forgotten, Your Highness."

Ryllis cursed to herself. *Silver.* She'd forgotten about the silver. Where was she to find something like that in a town where two crowns was wealthy? She followed Alessia back inside and watched her light the gas lamp next to an old wooden rocking chair. Her mother had owned a similar one . . . The memories, usually vague, were much too sharp to bear this time.

"You wouldn't believe how much people have been paying for her wool." Alessia pulled the hand spinner and a handful of pure white wool from a basket at her feet. Her smile became unfeigned. "And the milk is wonderful. So much that I can have it at every meal."

"I'm glad." Ryllis pulled up a stool to contemplate the silver problem—and how she remembered wanting milk at supper. "Has it helped things with your mother?"

Alessia's hands paused, and she looked at the floor. "A bit."

Well, no surprise there.

"I'm sorry," Ryllis replied. "I wish—" What was there to say?

"You've done what you could. I appreciate it, even if she doesn't." Alessia looked up. "What shall I do about the silver? There's no silver here, especially silver thread. Even the tavern down the street uses cheap stoneware for their glasses."

"I know." Ryllis rubbed her eyes. "Give me another moment. I'm trying to remember if there's something at the villa I could use." Since it didn't need to be *genuine silver*—just enough to fool Zaella.

"Excuse me, Your Highness," Wikström interrupted, dropping his jacket on the arm of Alessia's chair. "But I have something you might use."

They both stared at the silver thread that edged his collar and cuffs . . . and then Alessia laughed.

CHAPTER FOURTEEN

The mouse skull had taken little effort after all. A search of the alley nearest Alessia's house had turned up several in varying stages of decay—none of which Ryllis was willing to touch—but Wikström was not nearly as opposed to carrying it as she was. He'd shoved it in the pocket of his jacket, now missing the decorative trim around a cuff, then they'd both pretended it hadn't existed.

It was harder for her to ignore the fine yarn Alessia had spun in under an hour, pure white, shot with the silver-colored thread from Wikström's uniform. She ran it through her fingers, as he drove them back into the mountains, admiring the craftsmanship. It was a skill most young girls in Therus learned young, but without a mother to teach her . . .

Zaella certainly hadn't taught her anything useful.

The disquiet that had stalked her since they'd left Epuas returned as she considered what Zaella might have been teaching her *own* daughters. Had Bry and Greta known what their mother was? Worse, had they begun learning her ways? Outsmarting Zaella was one thing, but handling her and two more trained the same way? A shudder ran down her spine at the thought.

Wikström's disapproval was apparent as he stopped the car in front of the cottage, even if he hadn't said a negative word to her since leaving Alessia's house. Perhaps he believed she was beyond hope. But Ryllis didn't have time to worry about what he thought, since Zaella was waiting on the porch, like she'd known they were coming. Maybe she had. They'd driven right by the aspen circle, and whatever evil Zaella had stored there was powerful indeed. It would have to be to ensnare a telepath simply by allowing him to walk into the clearing.

A guarded smile crossed Zaella's face as Ryllis approached. "You were not to return except with what I asked for," she said.

"I have everything you wanted." Ryllis didn't return the expression. "Care to see?"

"Inside." Zaella waved her toward the door, sticking her arm out when Wikström made a move to follow. "Just her."

A daring move. Wikström started at the motion, like no one had ever refused him anything before—which was probably true —but Ryllis shook her head. It wasn't worth offending Zaella yet, not when she could change her mind about saving Kresten.

"Lieutenant—" Her voice shook. She hadn't realized how safe she'd felt with him at her side, and going into her former house alone with Zaella took every bit of her bravery and then some. "This shouldn't take very long. I'll be right back out. Everything will be all right."

He didn't look happy but didn't argue at her cautious promise. She held out her hand, and he placed the mouse skull in it, wrapped in silk. Zaella's gaze drifted down toward the package, and Ryllis clutched the silk tighter as she followed Zaella inside to the kitchen.

The house was chilly, even though the kitchen fireplace was stocked with fresh wood—Bry had to be upset about taking over what had once been Ryllis's chore—and the fire barely warmed the immediate area. But neither Bry nor Greta were anywhere to be seen this afternoon, and as Ryllis tried to catch her breath, the room remained silent except for the snapping and crackling of logs as they collapsed on the iron grate behind her.

"Lay them out." Zaella's order was cold as she settled into a faded wooden chair. "I want to see everything. No tricks."

Ryllis couldn't drop the mouse skull on the table fast enough. The yarn followed, Lavinia's snow-white wool interwoven with the silver thread. Not what Zaella had asked for, but maybe it was enough to fool her for a while. The violet—she hesitated a bit before pulling the violet from her pocket and laying it next to the yarn. Displaying her power still felt like a confession that could lead to her execution. Kresten said that fear would end in time, the more she used her powers in front of others, Vilarian and Cerethian alike, but he was wrong. The anxiety would never end.

Zaella's eyes widened at the brilliant color. "Fascinating." Her finger stroked the very edge of the bloom. "No wonder you married him—saving your own skin must have seemed very important."

As though she'd married Kresten to save herself. They'd have killed her, yes, but she had loved him so fervently she'd been terrified that he hadn't felt the same. That he'd only offered marriage out of pity. To have Zaella accuse her of using him . . .

"You have them, Zaella," she replied, struggling to keep an even tone. How in the Realm did Wikström expect her to just snatch everything from this woman? The timing would have to be perfect. And she had never been versed in such things. "Now set him free."

Zaella glanced up, but it appeared to be a struggle for her to move her eyes from the small pile.

"Set him free?" she asked in a sing-song voice, almost like she'd forgotten where she was.

"Do not play games with me." Ryllis forced her most imperial manner, the one Kresten always laughed at—not that his façade was much better, and he knew it. The fire still crackled behind her, but an icy feeling crept up her spine as she tried to push his memory from her mind. There were more urgent things to focus on now. "You promised."

"Ah, Ryllis." Zaella stroked the violets with her thumb, looking at them as she probably did a lover. "You're so trusting. So naïve. Even growing on a planet like Cereth, even seeing the things the Star Realm is capable of, even *experiencing* them, and you still believe people are inherently good. How foolish can you be?"

The ice turned to nausea as the kitchen closed in around her. Ryllis glanced toward the sink, searching for a glass, but there was nothing to wet her suddenly parched mouth. Moving toward it to look further would leave Zaella alone with the small pile.

"You understand I can't let him go now. He's too useful to me." Zaella brushed her thumb over her lips, like the violet had imparted its very essence. "These too. These violets . . . I don't know how they could have survived in this weather." She touched the flower once more. "It's amazing what you can do. I shouldn't have doubted your power, but you hid it so well."

Horror built inside Ryllis's soul, because she knew what Zaella meant. She *had* been foolish, and now—now there was no way to save Kresten. No way to prevent her from using these things, either.

"What do you mean you can't let him go?"

"I always doubted you could be this naïve, but it seems I was wrong once again." Zaella looked up and shrugged. "You know you weren't supposed to return."

"Return? To where? With these things? To Cereth?" Well, that made sense since no one had expected her to return to her home planet, but Zaella knew the Star Realm's decisions were beyond either of them. Realm's sake, they were beyond Kresten's wishes.

"I would think that's self-explanatory." Zaella's touch moved from the violet to the mouse skull. "There was supposed to be a blizzard. I had assumed you'd be so caught in looking for the violets that you wouldn't make it out of the mountains. I'd almost hoped for it, in fact—though you succeeding is a close second-best outcome, I'll admit."

Ryllis took a step backward, toward the fire. *Stupid.* She'd been so stupid to trust Zaella. And now Kresten would pay. She'd ruined everything. Ruined his life. Probably also ended her own. Zaella wouldn't try anything now, not with Wikström outside, but her chances of returning safely to Vilaria had just dropped.

"What do you plan on doing with these?" Ryllis asked weakly, gesturing to the table. She was afraid to know, but she had to stall somehow, had to come up with some plan. If only it was Kresten outside and she could speak telepathically with him. Intimate the bond might be, but it had definite practical uses.

"I haven't quite decided yet." Zaella didn't move her gaze from the trio of objects. "The mouse skull, provided by someone who's never otherwise seen death"—her fingers caressed it once more—"will be perfect for ending someone who's gotten in my way. Death begets death, you know. The wool, for staying warm this winter when I need to visit the aspen circle and draw from its strength. And the violet, well, I'll think of some use for it. Do you know assassins used to use this very type of violet to disguise the taste of poison?"

Evil.

Ryllis's hands shook. No matter how much she'd intended otherwise, she'd helped Zaella do evil, and Kresten would never forgive her for that, even if he wasn't in his right mind now. Even if the Fleet would come after him. He would have never wanted her to do this, even to save his own life.

Her muscles tensed, even though she couldn't stop shaking. Without thinking, she darted toward the table and swept the skull, violets, and wool to the floor like a petulant child, angry at the night's choice of supper. Zaella sat open-mouthed in the chair for the briefest of moments, then fell to her hands and knees, grasping wildly in front of her like the items were her last link to life itself.

Dropping to the floor in front of her, Ryllis grabbed the flower and the yarn from underneath Zaella's greedy palm, then sprang to her feet, grinding the skull to powder under her heel and dispersing it into a circle of dust. She unlatched the fireplace door with her other hand.

Zaella sat back on her knees and smiled up at her, her panic turning to a swift calm that made Ryllis's stomach turn.

"You won't do that," she said. "You don't want to destroy them, not really. Not after you spent so much effort finding them for me. Not after you kept that violet safe and living for so long—I know how your gift works. You belong to it as much as it belongs to you. Besides, you'll never know if I'm telling the truth about what I plan to do with them—or him. Save the flower and the wool, and maybe I'll save him." Her smile grew tighter. "What do you think you would do without him, foolish girl? Do you think they'd allow you to stay on Vilaria? They'd force you back to Cereth, where no one wants you. Do you think you'd survive here long on your own?"

She's lying. She's lying.

But the images careened through her mind, and though she didn't have the power of foresight, they were so vivid that she might well have developed it in the last thirty seconds. Moving from Kresten's beautiful flat. Leaving the flowers she'd so carefully cultivated there. No more trips to the mountains where they'd fallen in love—those memories would be taken as well, only to be replaced by a grim future on Cereth as a traitor. One who'd betrayed her planet then been discarded by the very empire she'd thrown in her lot with.

And no more—no more Kresten.

But perhaps that fate had already been decided. And since it had, there was nothing she could do but prevent Zaella from causing more misery.

With that, she yanked open the door to the fireplace. Flames shot to the top as she tossed the bundle in, Alessia's beautiful handiwork destroyed. Her chest threatened to collapse as she closed the door and stepped away.

"You stupid girl," Zaella snarled. The hatred in her expression faded as she stood, and Ryllis's heart beat harder at the obvious relief on her face. There was no reason Zaella should feel relief now—but then again, Ryllis had only slowed down her plans. Perhaps she had something worse in mind. "Do you think that matters? Do you think you stopped anything? Stopped me?"

"I know I stopped you from something. However large or small, I don't care. I know Kresten would be proud of me if you allowed him to be aware of it." She couldn't stop the sobs, but she didn't care what Zaella thought about the tears. "And the Fleet will stop you from whatever else you have planned."

With that, she walked to the front porch, Zaella screaming her name after her.

Wikström was there, his arms folded in that stance she knew so well by now. So was Bry, leaning against the railing, idly braiding her hair, and Ryllis pushed by her, suddenly ashamed of the tears. Wikström called her name as she headed to the car, and she stopped, not even knowing why.

"You were right, Lieutenant," she said, turning and running her fingers over her damp cheeks. Bry was following him, wide-eyed, and her shocked expression sent Ryllis's stomach into a freefall, like she'd dropped off a cliff deep in the forest. "It was a waste of time, a waste of hope. She was going to use what I brought her for—for horrible things. Things I should have known she was capable of, but I was too naïve. Or maybe I just didn't want to believe it. But I stopped her—for now."

Bry opened her mouth, then shut it.

"Bry—Bryony." She'd never called her stepsister by her full name. They'd never been close enough, and maybe it would enrage her now. But then again, maybe it would help. "You knew about her, didn't you?"

"Your Highness, she's practically a child," Wikström interrupted.

Ryllis shook off his words. Compassion, from a Shadow Force officer? Right now? Neither Bry nor Greta were *practically children*, anyway.

"But she knew," she replied. "Which means she might know a way to fix this. To free Kresten. One that doesn't involve unleashing more evil in these woods."

"I—" Bry looked at the ground, letting her as-yet-unbraided hair fall in her face. "I knew. But I don't know how to save him. Diviners aren't like you, with your innate gifts. You can tell if a person has potential, but they're not trained until they turn twenty, and—"

"And if this would have happened just a few years later, then you would have taken part in this macabre experiment of hers yourself. Bry, listen to me. You know what she's doing is wrong.

You know how much pain she's already caused this family, and you probably know about the other terrible things she's planning."

"You don't understand." Bry flushed, then her eyes grew glassy, like Ryllis's own tears were contagious. "No matter how old I was, or how much I knew or didn't know, she wouldn't have let me make that decision on my own. It wasn't as though I could have stopped her!"

"Then help us," Wikström said, his *practically a child* comment apparently forgotten if the abrupt frost in ·his voice was to be believed, "and I will do what I can to help you."

"I can't help you." The glassiness turned to tears, and she walked down the stairs, her hands held in front of her as if in appeal. Clearly Zaella had explained exactly what Shadow Force would do to her. To buy her silence, most likely. "I can't break her spell even if I wanted to. He entered the aspen circle, and there's nothing that can break that magic."

The aspen circle.

Ryllis grabbed her by the arm and pulled her away from Wikström. "Bryony—I know exactly how you can help."

CHAPTER FIFTEEN

Kresten pushed on the door of the telepathy room, then stopped and stared at his feet as the scent of sterile air washed over him. He shouldn't be doing this, for so many reasons. Camden was inside, strapped to a gurney, furious, and—if he still had half a brain left—terrified. Kresten was about to make that worse, and if there was one thing he had learned in the past few solar cycles, it was that he wasn't cut out for this anymore. He couldn't force his presence on yet another prisoner, couldn't condemn the guilty ones to what the Star Realm desired.

But his own guilt faded as the beeping of a machine somewhere inside the room caught his attention. Certainty took its place. He didn't want to do this job anymore, but Zaella wanted him to, and he would do whatever she needed. Needed her husband to be found guilty so she could move on. She'd told him so up in the cottage in the mountains, begged him to help her. He couldn't remember what she'd said Camden had done, but she'd said he was guilty, and so he was. The interrogation was only Shadow Force policy, and there was no question of what the outcome would be.

So, he stepped into the room and steeled himself. He'd done

this before, and he'd do it again. Fortunately, instead of a furious Camden, Granqvist was seated by the gurney, checking the flow of the drugs that kept Camden unconscious. Sedating a subject so early wasn't quite procedure, but apparently, Granqvist hadn't wanted to deal with his argumentativeness. Kresten couldn't blame him for that—Camden's attitude would wear on the most patient in Shadow Force.

"Wouldn't shut up," Granqvist said, as Kresten took his place on the other side and loosened his collar. "I knocked him out. You're all set—the authorization is on the datapad."

Kresten picked it up from the side table and flicked through the pages of authorization, verifying everything was in order before he signed. Even Shadow Force had rules. They were its own, of course, but they existed, and telepathic interrogation required the most bureaucracy of almost anything in the Star Realm. He handed the table back to Granqvist to sign as a witness, then leaned to the side and searched for a pair of gloves.

There were no cadre of medics in this garrison on Cereth as there were at Shadow Force headquarters on Vilaria, so he and Granqvist attached the electrode leads to Camden's head them-selves, testing each. It was a slow, painstaking process, since Granqvist had to stop several times to check each position in the manual, and Kresten remembered even less himself, but soon enough they were done. Belligerent or not, he wished he could have seen the fear on Camden's face.

"So that's it," he said, picking up a sanitizing wipe and washing it over Camden's skin.

If he's guilty.

Now where had that unwelcome thought come from?

Granqvist nodded and took the spent wipe from him, and Kresten flipped on the switch to start the tattoo machine. It hummed to life, and he picked up the pen, letting the weight settle in his hand. It felt unfamiliar, and he spun it around on his palm a few times before checking the settings. The last person he'd used this on . . . well, he couldn't remember the man's name. An Izonusian rebel, he'd been. What had happened to him after his telepathic confession? That would have been the Eradication Council's decision, and they showed little mercy toward insurgents.

He stuffed the guilt way down in his soul. This wasn't the time or the place for it, and the last thing he needed was to feel any pity for Camden. The man didn't stir as Kresten ran through the procedure in his head—it seemed Granqvist had been unnecessarily generous with the sedation. The pen heated, lights flashed, and with another deep breath, he placed the tip to Camden's forearm. Black ink seeped into his skin. He worked slowly, filling in half the first circle before he spoke.

"Might as well let him come out of it a bit," he said to Granqvist. "Won't matter in a few minutes, and I wouldn't want him to stop breathing before I can speak with him."

Granqvist made a noise of assent and adjusted a knob. Camden stirred a bit more, then settled, though his eyes didn't open. No matter. Shadow Force didn't care if the subject was aware of what was going on or not.

"You ready for them, Westermark?"

Kresten flinched as Granqvist's curious inquiry jerked him out of his stupor. Without realizing it, he'd almost filled in the entire circle without adding the nanobiotes. *Out of practice, I am out of practice.* He lifted the pen and wiped sweat away from his forehead with his bare wrist.

"Yeah," he replied, cursing the humidity that never seemed to stop invading the buildings in this part of Cereth. "Go ahead."

The machine grew high pitched as the nanobiotes flowed into the ink of the first circle. Kresten gripped the pen harder and started the second. Camden twitched, then moaned, but he ignored it. It would get worse for him. Always did. And Kresten would not let himself care this time. Proving Camden's guilt— that was all he cared about.

In the corner of his vision, Granqvist tightened the straps. "I don't like not having security in here," he said, glancing at the valve that would deliver more sedative.

"Mmm." What else was there to say? There was a guard outside the door, and that was plenty. Camden wasn't going anywhere, and Kresten wouldn't let Granqvist sedate him further, either. "Strange he hasn't reacted to them yet, though."

Granqvist coughed into his elbow. "It happens. Once I had a subject who took four unbroken circles before he even showed the slightest reaction to the nanobiotes. Strangest thing. I kept wondering if—"

Camden's scream of agony cut him off, and Kresten tried not to flinch in sympathy. His body remembered the pain, even if he couldn't consciously recall the memories of his training anymore. Searing fire, that was what he'd felt in his early Shadow Force training when he'd been subjected to the procedure. Some trainees felt electric shocks—probably most experienced it that way. Other subjects claimed to feel like they were being hit by clubs, though he'd never understood that.

He continued with the second mark, eyes downward as Granqvist continued his story of the man who'd taken four circles. Camden's screams grew louder, and as he convulsed, filling in the perfect circle became even more difficult. That, of course, was a measure of a Shadow Force telepath's skill, so Kresten gritted his teeth and focused, all too conscious of how Granqvist was watching him while he prattled away. Anyone who saw Camden after this would judge Kresten on his ability, and he didn't intend to humiliate himself with shoddy workmanship.

The second circle darkened, and Kresten lifted the pen for a third, then hesitated. Camden, according to Ryllis, had no innate gifts, no Vilarian blood, nothing that would imply he was resistant to telepathy, and so a third circle would be overkill. He set the pen down and watched the man convulse against the restraints for a moment, then met Granqvist's eyes over the shaking body.

"You're stopping?" Granqvist asked.

"Yeah." He stripped off the gloves and tossed them on the floor. "Going to try it now."

"He's still got quite a bit of brain activity." Granqvist shrugged and turned toward the monitors. "But it's your call."

"He shouldn't." Kresten stared at him for a moment. "Not anymore."

Granqvist frowned as his fingers traced along the screen. "Well, as long as you're aware, it probably doesn't matter."

Maybe. Maybe not. Kresten reached for the glass of water a tech had left on the side table and swallowed it in one gulp. The icy water slid down his throat, waking him up a bit, and he cracked his knuckles and leaned forward.

He'd done nothing more than brush his finger against the mark on Camden's skin when the odd sensation he'd felt at the house in the mountains threatened to overtake him. Heaviness, a weight that came from inside his own body, a dark, confusing mist that filled the room and clouded his vision.

He swore to himself and jerked his hand away from Camden's forearm.

"What happened?" The line between Granqvist's brows grew deeper. "You're not feeling bad already, are you?"

Realm's sake, why does everyone have to know about my headaches?

His frown matched Granqvist's as the weight of the question settled on to him.

A headache that he didn't actually have right now.

Strange.

"I—no." He wasn't feeling bad at all, and that didn't make any sense. "Not really. I suppose I'm just not used to this any longer— it's been a long while."

"We can cut this short." Granqvist peered at him, like he was wondering when he was going to have to lift Kresten off the floor. "I can try tomorrow."

The mist lifted, leaving him empty. Kresten grazed Camden's skin with a fingertip, but nothing happened. He was only imagining things, second-guessing skills he'd already honed.

"No. I'm all right. Let's get this over with." He looked up and forced a smile. "See you soon."

He placed his hand over the circles, covering them with his palm and fingers, then closed his eyes and pressed. Light flashed behind his eyelids, like they used to say it looked going through a wormhole, and all he could do was hang on as his power took him. The sensation wasn't unlike being flung through a wormhole either, and he focused on his breathing as he searched through the maze of nerves. The nanobiotes would lead him to Camden's mind to a certain extent—he could see their flashing and hear their silent chirping in the back of his own—but the rest was all on him.

He searched, wandered, meandered about through shadowy caverns and twisting corridors, feeling his way through a darkness heavier than space. A light appeared in the distance, the faintest of far-flung stars, and then there it was—a consciousness that wasn't his own. He reached out, tentatively, like he was taking the most fragile piece of crystal in existence into his hand.

Governor Camden? he asked. *Are you there?*

There was no immediate answer, and the silence gave him enough time to cringe. Calling Camden by his title was a mistake, but it was too late to do anything about it now, so he settled back into the darkness and waited. It was always strange to be the first one to speak, even stranger after only being in Ryllis's head for so long. But it wasn't as though a prisoner would know what they were feeling, so it was always the telepath who started the conversation.

At first, there was nothing but heavy inhalations, like Camden was trying to catch his breath. That wasn't surprising—happened every time. He wouldn't be in pain again until Kresten left his mind, but no doubt he was still trying to recover from the memory of the nanobiotes invading him. That happened, too, but Kresten immediately decided he was long over feeling pity for subjects.

Especially this one.

He waited in the silence of Camden's mind. Patience was something telepaths never expected to need when they joined Shadow Force, but so much of this work involved it. From waiting for an arrest, to waiting for a prisoner to speak during an interrogation, to waiting on the paperwork that never seemed to end . . . yes, he was an expert at patience now. Ryllis had helped him with that as well, even though he hated to admit she'd done anything good for him.

Captain Westermark?

Kresten jumped at the voice in his head, then remembered it wasn't an odd thing to be spoken to like this. No, the strangest part of all this entire experience, today, at least, was the confidence in Camden's voice. Except it was more than confidence, and the emotion confused him.

Could it be that he was hearing hope?

Of course not. That didn't make sense. Could Camden be this sure Shadow Force would never find out about his crimes? Some prisoners were that arrogant—more than some, really—but he'd still expected Camden to cave and confess immediately. Or simply refuse to speak.

I'm here, he replied. *Are you going to fight this, too?*

I'm not going to fight anything. I've been trying to get you inside my mind since I arrived here, but that blasted Fleet bureaucracy—I'm surprised any of you could put up with it with the way I've been acting. Camden paused and sucked in a breath, winded by his sudden rambling. *That woman did something to me. I have to say that before anything else, because you need to know. She did something to my mind, then blocked me from telling anyone.*

Kresten frowned, relieved as always that the subject couldn't tell his facial expressions.

Who did what? he asked.

Zaella. She's a sorceress. The words came rapidly now. *Enraptured me solar cycles ago, just after we married. Maybe before. I don't know. Everything is so fuzzy now.*

Kresten let a telepathic laugh echo through the connection. The accusation was ridiculous. Zaella, a sorceress? Camden was making things up. Fine. Kresten would have to do this the hard way, and that meant there would be no escaping the headache and blackout afterwards. He growled to himself, silently, then gritted his teeth as he reached out a tendril toward Camden's older memories.

You're lying, he replied. *And don't think I won't find out.*

Camden was silent for a moment.

Of course you'd say that. His earlier confidence disappeared, only to be replaced by desperation. *But that's because she did it to you, too.*

CHAPTER SIXTEEN

ikström remained outside the bare circle of trees —it was too dangerous for a telepath to be inside the aspens. Ryllis thanked the Light that Zaella had been brazen enough to boast about her accomplishment, since that saved Wikström from whatever would have happened. She could hear him pacing in the damp leaves, could feel the eyes of the aspens on her back, but she focused on Bry and drew herself upright. Someone had to be in charge, and the more she projected *Star Realm princess*, the more help Bry would be.

"Just to clarify, they all need to go," Ryllis said. Her heart ached at the very idea. "Right?"

Bry stared blankly off into the distance, looking like Kresten sometimes did when he was speaking telepathically. Ryllis doubted she was speaking to Zaella, but still, she wanted to shake her. They didn't have time for daydreaming.

"I—probably, yes," Bry stammered, bringing her focus back into the circle. "I don't know for sure, so that would be safest."

"And just cutting down the trees will do it?" She'd suspected as much, but now that they were here in the woods, with dark clouds gathering in the gloomy sky above, it was difficult to believe it could be that easy. "That will destroy her power? Free Kresten?"

And maybe Alder as well.

"I don't know!" Bry's shoulders tensed, and her frustrated scream echoed across the top of the mountain. "You've got to believe me!"

Wikström took a step forward.

"Out! I don't even want you touching them, Lieutenant, much less stepping inside this circle. We'll handle it." Ryllis pointed a finger at him, and he lurched backward, into the pine trees and bare maples. "All right, Bry. We're going to try."

She hefted up the ax and cursed Kresten's protectiveness over the past solar cycle. She hadn't done manual labor since before her imprisonment on Cereth, and the lack of exercise had made her weak. Planting flowers had healed her mind, but not her muscles.

Bryony picked up the second axe and tested her swing against one of the thicker aspens. Ryllis already doubted she'd be much use, but she had to be better than no help at all.

"Let's start with the thicker ones, and move on to the thinner ones," Bry said. "They'll be easier, in case we tire out too soon."

Ryllis nodded, brushed her fingers against the trunk of the largest tree, then lifted her axe and swung it. Maybe her stepsister really wanted to help.

Believing otherwise was unbearable.

Ryllis was sweating, despite the snow landing on her shoulders. Fifteen of the aspens lay on their sides in the dirt, but another three stood, snowflakes drifting through their empty branches. She and Bry had taken turns chopping and acting as lookouts while Wikström paced around the outside, choosing their next target.

He'd wanted to chop a few himself, but Ryllis had declined once more, unsure if even touching the trees would be harmful for him. The last thing she and Bry needed—the last thing the Star Realm needed—was for Zaella to end up with another Shadow Force officer under her control. Not that she cared what the Star Realm needed, but she cared about saving Kresten.

Bry leaned against the first tree and wiped her brow. Snowflakes dotted her dark hair, melting a second after they fell.

"I don't know if I can do it anymore. We should have brought Greta."

"You have to do it—and Greta's too young for this." Ryllis picked up the ax and swung it against the farthest tree from the road. It might have been one of the thinner aspens, but the blade scarcely made a dent in the trunk this time, and her muscles were screaming in agony. Strangely, though, her soul was not. Perhaps the evil that the tree held mitigated the loss she should have felt. "Sit there and rest a bit while I work on this one, but we'll need to work together on the last two."

Bry slid to the ground and put her head in her hands.

"I'm sorry," she muttered. "I'm so, so sorry."

"For what?" The blade stuck in the tree, and Ryllis yanked it out, then dropped it to the ground. It was too heavy to hold unless she was actively swinging it. Everything was too heavy now, even her arms—if only she could drop *them*.

"For being awful for you for so long. For listening to the things Mother said about you, and treating you like a servant, and gossiping about you, and worse of all, I suppose—for believing that you deserved it all."

"Bry, you don't need to worry about that." Ryllis dragged the axe from the ground and swung it at the aspen. "I will not turn you in to the Star Realm, and neither will Lieutenant Wikström. You don't need to apologize because you feel threatened by me or Kresten."

"You can call me Bryony, you know. I don't mind. To tell you the truth, I've been wanting you to, but I knew it was something I could never ask for after everything that happened." Bry's shoulders sagged. "And I'm not afraid of His Highness. I meant what I said. I know this isn't an excuse, but I hope you'll see it as the explanation it is: I was young. I missed Father, and I resented you for having one when I didn't. And I knew Mother was capable of things that—well, let's just leave it at *things*. I suppose you know what those things are now. So, when she accused you of enchanting the cow or causing the vegetables to whither, I took my fear of her powers out on you."

The notch had grown as Bry spoke, and Ryllis took a step away from the trunk to catch her breath. It couldn't be a long break, since the tree was waving in the breeze, becoming a hazard to all three of them, but she could barely move any longer. If only Wikström could be trusted to knock it down. She'd beg for his help if she could.

"Bry, you don't—" What had Kresten told her, so long ago, when she'd confessed, however inadvertently, to not trusting his father? "I understand why you did what you did. And now all's forgiven. Truly."

"But they're going to take her away, aren't they?" Genuine pain crossed Bry's face for the first time. Well, of course. She loved her mother, however much evil she'd performed.

"She enchanted a Shadow Force officer," Ryllis replied, focusing. "A prince of the Star Realm. I can't imagine—"

She cut herself off. Bry didn't need to know details. It was enough that she herself knew what the Fleet would do to Zaella, and deserved or not, the fate made her shudder. A suppression chip—did those even work on sorceresses?—then captivity on some prison asteroid, far away from any inhabited planets. The Star Realm didn't play around with subjects gifted with any kind of power, and they certainly didn't show mercy to ones who took malevolent powers for their own.

Bry nodded and put her head back on her knees, and Ryllis,

too exhausted to comfort her, picked up the axe again. Tree after tree fell to the cold ground, until a single aspen stood, its eyes focused on her. Ryllis didn't give that much notice in return, just struck at it over and over, until it crashed on the ground.

In the golden silence, the thing she'd feared the most embraced her.

Nothingness.

No bolt of lightning struck the ground, no rush of birds overcame them, no clouds darkened the sky overhead.

Nothing had changed.

Which meant there was no hope for Kresten.

CHAPTER SEVENTEEN

Zaella did what? In the maze of Tavis Camden's mind, Kresten scoffed at his claim. Desperate men always came up with the strangest stories—did he really think anyone in Shadow Force would ever believe something this ridiculous? *Enraptured me?* he went on. *I doubt she's capable of that.*

You've got to understand. Camden's request was more like a plea. *She did this to you, I swear it.*

Kresten scooted back in his chair as far as he could without removing his hand from the mark, then rolled his eyes in Granqvist's direction, even though everything outside of Camden's mind was a gray, misty haze. He'd forgotten about this part, too—how he scarcely existed in the real world anymore.

Explain, he ordered.

She's a sorceress. What else do you want me to say? I don't know how she did it, not exactly, but she did. You're a telepath—I assume it must have been easy for her.

Kresten let out a light telepathic laugh. *Sorcery is banned in the Star Realm, and you know it. Has been for a thousand solar cycles.*

As though that stops the ones who want to practice it, especially in the mountains of Cereth. Camden huffed, then swore. *You know I'm right. I know she still has control of you.* He paused, then his mind grew quiet. *I thought this would be enough to force my way through,* he added, though it didn't seem to be directed at Kresten.

You thought wrong, Kresten replied, though he didn't have the faintest idea what Camden was talking about. No matter. He'd search his deeper memories later, the ones even Camden had forgotten. *Now—let's talk about your calendar.*

My calendar? Camden's surprise didn't sound feigned.

The one with resistance meetings on it. Handwritten—in your handwriting, I might add. You know, the one you didn't want to talk about earlier. The one you were so defiant about that you almost got yourself beat up.

Camden's mind grew dark, like the evening shadows in the mountains. That wasn't unusual during a telepathic interrogation, but it meant Kresten was on the wrong track, had taken a wrong turn somewhere, asked the wrong question. The man truly was confused, and telepathic confusion could be contagious. Kresten moved to rub his eyes, forgetting it wouldn't do a bit of good for his fatigue as long as he was this wound up in someone else's thoughts.

I—the tendrils of synapses in Camden's mind became coiled and murky, adding to the disorientation. *I don't have a handwritten calendar.*

You can argue with me all you want, but it won't do any good. I can read your unconscious thoughts . . . or didn't they tell you that?

Camden became silent.

Good, then. You stop talking and let me look around.

It was more of an order than was needed, but Camden's consciousness faded a bit from the forefront of Kresten's own mind. He poked a bit, but the governor remained silent and still, so he skimmed over his recent memories. There *was* a calendar there. He could see it on a desk, could see the trees outside the cottage through the window, could see Camden's hand reaching for it. Could see . . . was the man frowning at it?

Kresten gasped for air. Beyond the veil where the real world remained, Granqvist moved on the other side of the gurney, and the motion made him sick to his stomach. He gestured with the hand that wasn't touching the ink on Camden's arm, and Granqvist stilled. He could pull him off the floor when he was done.

Cautiously, with the remembrance of his own blackouts fading away, he returned to Camden's memories. The governor had picked up the small paper calendar—black cover, no date or pattern on it—and turned it over in his hands, muttering under his breath. Flipping through it, he'd frowned again, but Zaella had called his name before he'd comprehended any of the words inside.

Zaella.

Her name centered him once more, chasing away the remaining nausea. Right. Now he remembered his goal. He had to prove Camden guilty. Had to follow through on his promise to her. Had to—

A supernova exploded in his head, showering light through his entire body. Violating every protocol he'd ever been taught, he grasped at his forehead, leaving Camden untouched. Pain? No. It felt like he should be in pain, but there was nothing, only that blasted flickering luminosity.

What in the Realm?

He shoved his hand back on Camden's forearm. The connection hadn't been severed, and he was thankful for that. He was still in the man's mind, but everything was clear now. Like the water in the clean mountain lake. He hadn't even realized it before, had been too out of practice with telepathic interrogation, but that same haze that had hung around him in Camden's house had surrounded his mind, even if he hadn't realized it.

Find what you were looking for?

Camden's question was a sneer. Maybe the man was just a jerk.

Zaella. It was becoming hard to breathe, and Kresten hesitated to catch his breath. Camden could see that weakness, connected as they were, and he'd use it against him. *Tell me—tell me more. About what she did to me?*

You're willing to listen to me now?

Yes. I want to know. Something just happened—something snapped. A light, then everything became clear.

She lost her hold on you. Camden sighed, then went on. *We'd been married only a solar cycle. She was . . . I loved her. But then things changed shortly afterward. She became secretive, short with me. I'd find her in the barn, just sitting there in the dirt with her eyes closed. At first, I thought she was unhappy with our marriage, although she claimed she wasn't. And she became short with Ryllis. I was angry at first, and then eventually, it all just made sense. Ryllis was upset about her mother, upset I'd remarried, and she took that out on Zaella and her daughters. I had no choice but to discipline her, and after that, things grew worse.*

A twinge of pain spread through Kresten's heart, and he didn't care if Camden could feel it.

She didn't take anything out on Zaella, Kresten replied. *That's not Ryllis, and I think you know it. She's more apt to go isolate herself in the garden than cause problems at home.*

No. I understand that now. But I saw it—it didn't make any sense in my mind, but I swear I saw the way she was treating Zaella and her daughters. But only while Zaella was around. Whenever I went to the office, all I could think about was getting back home and seeing Ryllis. And then, suddenly, one day I couldn't even think about that.

What changed your mind?

When Ryllis arrived—something, I don't know. Zaella's power must have cracked, and even though I couldn't speak, I knew the truth in my mind. But I knew whatever spell she'd put me under wouldn't allow me to speak it. I didn't know if I could speak about it telepathically, but it was my last chance. I was an ass, yes. As much as I could be without appearing an obvious traitor. I wanted you to become suspicious enough to be forced to read my mind, not execute me outright.

Camden drew another breath, as if the speech had taken everything out of him. In the corner of Kresten's eyes, Granqvist moved again.

You love her, Kresten said.

*So much. My girls were my life, especially my Ryllis. She still is, in whatever corner of my mind Zaella hasn't touched yet. When I think of the accusations I made, what she went through because of me—*His voice broke, as much as a voice in one's mind could. *I love her so much.*

But once we're done here, you won't remember how you really feel about her. Kresten wanted to vomit all over the floor. How was he supposed to tell Ryllis what had happened to her father, that he wasn't the bastard everyone thought he was, even though there wasn't a thing anyone could do to fix him? *You won't remember that it's Zaella controlling your mind.*

You've been freed. For the second time, hope wound its way through Camden's mind. *Maybe, whatever happened affected her hold on me as well.*

Maybe. He pushed Camden's emotion away. *You're tired, aren't you?*

Yes. Is it almost over?

It wasn't a surprise. Telepathic interrogation exhausted the subject, too, but there was still work to do. Camden needed to be cleared of everything now that the process was underway. It had become a disaster of an investigation, and now there would be charges of partiality and of Realm knew what else, but if nothing else, Granqvist's presence would keep him honest.

I can do the rest without your help, he said, *if you relax and don't fight me. It can be fast, but I need to verify the accusations Zaella made are completely false. I—I'm sorry. It's for the best if there are no questions about your innocence.*

Camden made a mumble of assent, then his mental presence faded away into a jumble of thoughts and memories. At first it was all noise to Kresten, bright and loud and unpleasant, but it was familiar somehow. Comfortable. Just like he had with every other prisoner, he picked through each tendril of thought, stretching them into words, searching for patterns, twisting the memories into images.

It was, though he hated to admit it to himself, something he was good at. Something the Fleet needed him for. He'd always been respectful, anyway, and that was something not all Shadow Force officers were capable of.

But he couldn't keep doing this. It wasn't what he wanted. He'd sworn as much in front of his father, and that was how he knew he really meant it.

Focus.

Camden jerked at the order that wasn't for him at all. Kresten sent a burst of tranquility through the telepathic connection, and the man stilled immediately, his mind blank again. By the Realm, he wanted to sever connection and think through his own situation, but he continued to pry, continued to search.

There was nothing. The calendar? Wikström might have found it in Camden's house, but Kresten was nearly certain now that the governor hadn't had a thing to do with it. He could *feel* Camden's confusion over its appearance, could hear the questions he'd asked Zaella—who, true to form, had made up a story. The gray mist he'd felt in the house surrounded Camden in his memories, and then he was sure.

The governor was innocent.

Whether he'd remain in his position after this was still a question—the Star Realm treated even exonerated prisoners as guilty, after all—but he would be freed. He would never stand in front of the Eradication Council, would never be forced from Cereth. Kresten could tell Ryllis of that result with great relief, even if he couldn't give her father back to her.

He swallowed and backed just slightly out of Camden's mind.

Governor? All done. Can you hear me?

Now— A hint of fear touched Camden's voice for the first time. *Now what happens?*

I leave you alone and give you your mind back. You'll wake up, pain meds and all. I'll write a report. And you—you'll be freed.

And Ryllis? Zaella?

Kresten sighed out loud. *I'll tell Ryllis what happened here, every bit. I can't promise it'll help anything with her, but if I know her at all, it will. Even if Zaella's hold on you doesn't release, I know Ryllis will forgive you. Shadow Force will arrest Zaella, of course.*

He would not be the one to interrogate her, thankfully. If history held, Granqvist would pull him off the floor in a few minutes, and then he'd have earned himself a long respite. After that? Realm's sake, no one in Shadow Force would want to risk dealing with her.

That's all you can do. And I'm grateful for that, Your Highness.

I wish I could do more. Now relax. The worst part's over.

Kresten wound his way back through Camden's nerves, toward the black circle, toward reality. It took forever, which meant he'd been in his mind longer than usual, and that meant that what was coming would be . . .

No, he wouldn't think about what that meant yet. Effervescence flashed about him, a clamor of blues and the brightest white he'd ever seen, but he focused on the circle, dangling out there in the distance like the restful sight of a planet after too many wormhole jumps. Closer and closer it became, and when he was close enough, he removed his hand from Camden's forehead, then blinked.

"Westermark?" Granqvist's voice was loud, like the rockets on an ancient starship.

Kresten waved him off and pressed his eyes closed. "I'm here. Just give me a minute. And Realm's sake, lower your voice, would you?"

The soft sounds of the life support machines reverberated throughout the room. He blinked one more time, but he was still sitting upright on the stool by the bed, could still see and hear. Risking both his balance and pride, he looked up. Granqvist was eyeing him with no small bit of apprehension from the opposite side, though to his credit, he didn't rush over and force Kresten to lie down on the floor.

"You're awake," he said instead. "I was under the impression that would not happen."

"You aren't the only one." Kresten pushed himself to his feet and tested his balance. No headache, no dizziness. Perhaps he'd stay conscious after all. He glanced at Camden, his eyes still closed, breath shallow but regular. "How's he doing?"

"Resting comfortably." Granqvist checked the monitors once more. "So? How awkward is this going to be for the Star Realm?"

Kresten couldn't help the broad grin that spread across his face. "You're going to want to sit down before we bring him out of it—because you're not going to believe this."

CHAPTER EIGHTEEN

Wikström had escorted her into an office somewhere in Fleet base that might as well have been a maze, brought her a cup of tea, then disappeared. However helpful he'd been earlier, Ryllis didn't miss his company, but the silence was deafening—and too close to the memories of her own arrest. She paced, tapped her fingers on the bare desk, and tried to braid her dirty hair a half dozen times, then gave up and allowed it to spill over her shoulders.

Before setting the steaming cup on the table in front of her, Wikström had said that Kresten wanted to see her. Had news for her, though he hadn't elaborated on what that news might be. She couldn't imagine. It had to be something about her father, but whether that was good or bad—

You're being foolish.

Of course it was bad. The Fleet had arrested him, Shadow Force had probably telepathically interrogated him by this point, and since he was important in the Star Realm puppet government, they wouldn't risk making any mistakes. They'd have to do things exactly according to procedure, and that never ended well, even if she'd escaped the worst. She was angry with her father, yes, but did he deserve this?

There wasn't any immediate answer to that question, so she pulled the chair up to the desk and put her head down. No one could be allowed to see her cry, and even though the Fleet wouldn't dare place a princess of the Vilarian Star Realm under video surveillance, she wouldn't take the chance someone had made a mistake, forgotten to turn the camera off. Exhaustion and misery and fear combined, and the tears fell then, dampening her sleeve. She wanted to be off Cereth, back in Kresten's mountains on Vilaria, free from the memories and the pain.

"Are you crying?"

Ryllis jerked her head up. Kresten stood in the doorway, his hands in his pockets and a frown on his face. He took a step toward her as she stood, then stopped, as if he wasn't quite certain how to react to her very existence. She wasn't certain, either. If chopping down the trees hadn't worked . . .

"Darling star—"

He said nothing else. Couldn't, because she wrapped her arms around him, and squeezed, unwilling to let go. Her tears were going to ruin his uniform, but she didn't care. She only cared that he was standing here, looking like he used to, calling her the endearment he and no one else was allowed to, and that he was letting her hold him. His hand ran up and down her back, and she could only sob at his touch.

"I didn't think I'd ever see you again." She dragged the words from her soul, the fear of failure too vivid. *Cutting down the trees worked.* "Not the real you."

"It did. Wikström told me all about it, and I only wish I had been there to see it." He ran his fingers down her damp cheek. "Ryllis, I—I wish I'd known how horrid I was acting toward you. Realm's sake, I love you so much, and I can scarcely understand it myself. That hold she had over me—I'm ashamed of the things I've said, the things I've *thought*."

Things you will never hear from me, he added in her mind. *Please don't ask what kinds of evil went through my mind over the past few days. You don't deserve that pain, and I refuse to subject you to it.*

"It's not your fault." She tried to laugh, but the things he'd said in that house in the mountains were still too raw to find amusing. "But don't you ever fall under a spell ever again."

Kresten's eyes crinkled as he leaned toward her. "I am most certainly not planning on it."

His lips met hers before she could blink. The intensity of his kiss left no doubt—this was her Kresten. The Kresten she'd fallen in love with and promised to grow old with. His touch made her helpless in his arms, and not only was she unable to argue with that, she didn't want to. His hands were in her hair—they were always in her hair, now that it was long enough to wind his fingers through—and she found her own stroking the back of his neck, simply *experiencing* him like she had back when he'd first kissed her like this.

I could hold you like this forever. He spoke silently, but his lips were against her ear, and she shivered. *But there's something you need to see.*

"Now?" she murmured in return, one palm against his chest, the other arm around him. *I'm afraid I can't let go of you. Not now. Whatever it is will simply have to wait.*

Kresten backed away and held up a finger, threatening and promising at the same time. Ryllis tilted her head at him, but he only smiled as he pushed the door open and motioned outside. A fraction of a second later, a figure appeared, and her heart threatened to stop.

Father.

She blinked at him, wordless.

Why is he here?

The thought wasn't meant for Kresten, and he seemed to know, for he didn't say a word as she stared at her father. He was dressed in the gray prison uniform she was too familiar with and still hated. Two black circles marched up his forearm. He looked old, or maybe tired. Not the man who'd tossed her in the air to make her laugh as a child, and not the man who'd called her useless and weak as an adult. He just looked . . .

Sad.

Beaten.

And she felt . . . at first, she couldn't figure out what she was feeling.

Compassion?

She glanced at Kresten, and he lifted his shoulders in feigned embarrassment, sending a burst of reassurance into her mind at the same time.

"Surprise," he said. "Zaella—well, let's just say you and your father have a lot of catching up to do."

Her hand hit her mouth in realization, horrible and wonderful all at once.

"She did it to you, too?" she asked. "All those horrible things you said and did to me?" Her eyes were still wet, and it was humiliating to show emotion like this, but she'd cried in front of Kresten before. And now there was no stopping it. "Turning me in to the Fleet? Having me sent to Vilaria? Zaella made you do that?" It was too much to hope for, but he nodded, and her heart beat again.

"And I wish there was something I could do to take it all back. We've wasted so much time, Ryllis, and I don't intend to waste any more."

She flew at him and threw her arms around him, hesitating for only a fraction of a second as her gaze caught the circles. "Not any longer. Never again."

Father stroked her hair as she sobbed. "No. Never again. Though it seems—and I'm sorry for what I said when he told me about you two—that you've found happiness after everything. I am glad for that, if you'll believe me this time. And I hope you'll always be as happy as I know you are with him right now."

Without moving her head from his shoulder, she reached for Kresten's hand. "He's a good man, Father."

"For a Vilarian, she means to say," Kresten broke in.

Her tears flowed even harder when she burst into laughter. "His sense of humor could use a little finessing, though," she said in return. "Or maybe just his timing. But we can work on that, now that he's in control of his own mind again."

Kresten squeezed her hand, then backed away to perch himself on the table. Father put his hands on her shoulders and looked her up and down with a smile.

"You're so grown up." His face fell a bit. "And a princess. One who sounds, if you'll excuse me, like she's been living on Vilaria for some time."

"I'm the same person. Just with prettier dresses." She looked down at her muddied pants and forced a chuckle. Chopping down the aspens had destroyed her clothes. "Well, sometimes."

"You cut down the trees," Father said in awe, with just a glance at the dirt. "Ryllis, I don't know how I can ever repay you for that."

"I had help from Bry, and I swear, she wanted them gone as much as I did." Kresten shifted in her peripheral vision, and she hurried onward, desperate to explain. Bry deserved as much protection as she could give now. "She knew about Zaella, but Father—Kresten—she's young, and she's terrified of her mother. There was nothing she or Greta could have done to stop her. They could only protect themselves."

"Wikström told me—he talked to her earlier." Kresten's tone grew serious. "And I don't see any reason the Fleet needs to know anything different."

"Thank you." The relief made her sick. She staggered backward against his side, and he wrapped his arm around her. "But now what?"

"What do you mean?" Kresten asked.

"What will happen to Bry and Greta?"

Her father glanced at Kresten. "If the Star Realm will allow it, I'd like to retire. Bry and Greta are welcome to the house in the mountains, if they'd be willing. I've no desire to return."

"I'm not so sure they'd want to stay there, either." She glanced at Kresten. "Do you think they'd be willing to stay with us, even come to Vilaria when your assignment ends?"

"Well, why don't we ask them?"

He unwound himself from her and knocked on the door. Bry pushed it open, Greta behind her. Greta's hand was stuck firmly in Bry's, and both their eyes were wide as they landed on Kresten and then the rest of the room. Here on a military base controlled by their enemy, they looked like children, and it was only her uncertainty of their wishes that kept Ryllis from hugging them both.

Bry glanced from her to Kresten, like she couldn't decide what to do.

"Your Highness," she began, "I am so sorry. I beg—"

"Don't." Kresten held up a hand. "Please. None of that is necessary—it's time to move forward."

Bry's confused gaze moved to Ryllis.

"It's over," she said gently. "And what happens now is up to you. My father has offered his home, if you'd like—though I'd quite understand if you wanted a fresh start. If so, you're more than welcome on Vilaria. There's space enough anywhere you choose to go, and we"—she squeezed Kresten's hand, and his ensuing smile made her knees weak—"would be thrilled to have you stay with us for as long as you need."

"But why?" Greta moved a bit from Bry's protective stance. The two words were the most she'd spoken to Ryllis in a dozen solar cycles. "We were horrible to you."

"Because you're still my sister. You had no chance of treating me with any respect after what Zaella told you about me and what she did to my father, and I can't hold that against you."

"But Vilaria is—you are—" Bry stared at her. "I don't think I can live in a palace."

Kresten burst into laughter. "Ryllis, is this the point where I tell her my flat is too small for four people, and that we'll need to find something more suitable? Not a palace. Something casual and still too small for imperial siblings to visit. Maybe somewhere near Arvika University? I've always loved the parks and creeks there."

"Arvika University?" Greta gasped. "But that's only for Vilarians."

"And off-worlders who have someone to pull strings for them, and if the university can't accept a recommendation from the imperial family, then I'm not sure what use my station actually is." He glanced at Father, who was barely standing. "But we can discuss details later. Governor Camden needs to get cleaned up and rest, and Ryllis and I need to speak alone. The guard outside will escort you somewhere more appropriate."

She wanted to hug Father one more time, but he bowed to Kresten and gestured Bry and Greta out before she could move toward him. Kresten motioned her back into her chair and perched on the table again, that contemplative look that both frightened and intrigued her on his face.

"What?" she asked, not wanting to know the answer. "Haven't we discussed everything already?"

"I need you to hear me out," he replied, tapping an anxious fingertip on the table. "Before you say anything."

"You're worrying me."

Did you lie before? Is Bry still in trouble? Is Father truly not free?

"No, no, and no. It's something else, but it's also your decision to make for me." He ran his hands over his face and sighed, then slid to the empty chair next to her. "Ryllis, I—I want to rejoin the Fleet."

The small room grew stifling hot in a heartbeat.

"Rejoin the Fleet?" she stammered. "Kresten—"

"Hear me out." He grabbed her hands. "When I was speaking to your father, I realized something—they need me. Realm's sake, they need anyone who's been off Vilaria, who understands there's more to the galaxy than the home world and doing the will of my father."

Her brows creased. "You aren't doing the will of your father?"

"Well, he thinks I am." Chagrin flashed in his expression. "But I'm my own person, and I can enact change, even if only a bit, and slowly. I can't do that as a minor prince who'll never take the throne, but I can do it here, even if it's only by treating a prisoner with respect. Even if it's only by showing Shadow Force that off-worlders aren't the enemy they think. Even if it's only by showing my colleagues I understand the sacrifices they're making."

It all made sense. Kresten was compassionate, even to prisoners and slaves, and more than that, he was married to her—one of those off-worlders, always under suspicion by their Vilarian masters, never quite treated as a full member of the Realm. And by volunteering for work made redundant by his position in the imperial family, he showed he cared about his colleagues, too. His colleagues who had no choice but to join Shadow Force or face imprisonment.

"How am I to argue with that kind of sacrifice?" She reached for his cheek with a finger, and he drew her close. "You've made it impossible."

You can argue as much as you want, and I'll listen as long as you need me too. And if you truly can't accept it, then I'll find something else to do.

It scares me. She pressed her cheek against her chest. *It's not what I was expecting you to say, not the life I was expecting at the end of this visit. That last solar cycle on Vilaria, just the two of us—I was happier than I ever imagined I could be, and the idea of losing that breaks my heart.*

And I somehow suspect you didn't think you'd end up a princess when you were forced to leave Cereth, he replied. *Yet somehow that part of the situation worked out just fine.*

Ryllis laughed into his mind. *That it did.*

So? I won't do this without your blessing.

She took a deep breath. *I don't know how I can love you more for deciding this, but I do. Most wouldn't give up your kind of life for this.*

To be fair, I'm not giving anything up immediately. You've forgotten the emperor has me trapped for a while on Cereth. If you thought this assignment ended with the resolution of your father's case, well . . . you haven't figured him out yet.

I doubt I ever will. And after that?

Whatever Shadow Force decrees. I would assume back to Vilaria for a while. Kresten's fingers wound through her hair. *But let's just enjoy today for now, no?*

Just today?

Greedy. His telepathic laugh made her shiver. *And the next hundred solar cycles, if you insist.*

Oh, yes. I insist.

Good. Because—

Ryllis pressed her lips against his and cut off his protest. "Kresten," she said, "No more planning."

I had plans for tonight. He pulled away and tilted his head toward the ceiling, a light playing on his face. *But you know, that's fine. If you don't want to hear about the dinner under the stars—the flowers—the rose-scented bath, lit by a roaring fire . . .* He laughed. *But you're right. No more planning.*

Kresten!

He was silent for a moment. *I suppose it'll have to wait until tomorrow, since security found a trespasser halfway up one of the olive trees earlier today. Naked.*

Her hand hit her mouth. *Alder?*

Who's Alder?

Long story. Ryllis laughed. *Maybe I'll tell you sometime. But you don't have to make anything up to me, Kresten.* She threw her arms around him and laid her head against his chest. *Because I love you —and I always will.*

EPILOGUE

*A*steroid 287X was dark.

The landing pad was lit by a single fluorescent bulb, the corridors were bleak, and the control room was filled with red light to protect the guards' night vision. Even in the medical bay, where Zaella lay unconscious under harsh white lights, the shadows crept in from the corners, threatening and cruel. Arms folded, Kresten watched from the side as the medic checked the position of the suppression chip once more, then placed a bandage over the wound.

"Records say it's been almost a hundred solar cycles since, uh, an unnaturally gifted prisoner was here." The medic pulled off his gloves and tossed them into a dim corner toward what Kresten assumed was a trash receptacle. "It's an interesting change from all the rest. Not that it matters, I suppose," he chattered on. "They require little care. Toss a bit of food in every so often, make sure they're not hypoxic—but even that's taken care of by sensors in the cells. Easy duty station, you know?"

Kresten didn't reply. It was difficult enough knowing a half dozen other prisoners were here for no other reason than an unfortunate quirk of their birth.

Ryllis would have been imprisoned in one of these cells.

It was that thought that stayed with him as he and Granqvist escorted Zaella's floating gurney through the dim corridor to her new home. His boots clanked on the open steel that allowed atmosphere to flow freely between compartments, but other than that and Granqvist's occasional cough, the cell block was silent, the feeling of hopelessness too heavy to bear.

"Here we are." Granqvist fumbled in his pocket for the visitor's security token he'd been given at the control center—even Shadow Force officers weren't trusted with permanent access here—and pressed it against the door's security pad. "Mrs. Camden's new home."

Kresten slid the door open and stared inside. Dark steel lined a box perhaps ten paces deep by ten paces wide. A line of light came from around the edge of the ceiling, and though his eyes adjusted, it was no match for the feel of sunlight on one's face. Empathy was more of a curse than most realized, and he felt that curse now—so did Granqvist, he thought, when he glanced at him.

"Well, let's do it," he said, reminding himself for the hundredth time that if anyone deserved this, it was Zaella. They weren't leaving Ryllis here, and so he would do his duty.

The gurney didn't fit inside, so they slid Zaella's limp body onto the floor, then stepped outside and replaced the force field. She stirred at the disruption, then shifted, eyes blinking furiously. No surprise. She'd been unconscious since Cereth, and it always confused prisoners to wake up on 287X. The medic had said so, at least, and Kresten had no reason to doubt him.

"What—" she began.

"Welcome to Asteroid 287X."

Granqvist's tone wasn't quite heckling, but Zaella gasped, then dragged herself to her knees and stared at them both. In less than a fraction of a second, she must have figured out where she was, because her expression turned from confusion to hate.

"You won't get away with this," she snarled through the force field. "You have no idea—"

"Your powers are gone." Kresten couldn't help a small smile. "You won't be using them for evil any longer."

"Bastard. Liar." She took a breath. "*Vilarian.*"

A longer string of curses in a language he didn't understand fell from her mouth then—not the vulgar kind Kresten had ever heard from men in the Fleet. No, these must have been the ones in that book in the barn, the ones Zaella must have spoken in the aspen circle to consolidate her power there, the ones she must have spoken over Camden and used for whatever other nefarious activities she'd done. He didn't want to know what those were. Figuring what wickedness Zaella had done was someone else's problem now. Maybe no one's. The Star Realm had placed her here for a reason.

"Feel better?" he asked when she fell silent.

Her rage slid into a malevolent smile.

"You don't want to leave me here alone, Captain Westermark. You won't." Her hands moved in the shadows, though he couldn't see what spell she was trying to work with her fingers. Kresten had to give her credit—she was persistent. "Remember what you promised me? That Camden would suffer for all the things he'd done, and then we'd be together? You can still have that." She closed her eyes and muttered under her breath, words Kresten couldn't understand and didn't want to.

"Let's go," he said to Granqvist. "All done here."

Granqvist nodded, and as they turned to go, Zaella's mutterings stopped.

"You Vilarian dog!" The sudden scream echoed in the empty corridor, clanging off the steel walls and diffused, bare lights. "You can't do this. Do you even know who I am? What kind of power I wielded until you brought me here? I turned that cheating bastard Alderson into a mouse—do you know what I can do to your wife? To you?"

The screams, frantic and haphazard, seemed to strike him on the back as he continued walking, gaze on his boots. Triumph flitted around in his mind, yes, but this place weighed on him. They said he'd eventually get over it, but maybe they lied about that. As Zaella's screams grew fainter, the surrounding misery grew.

Damn empathy.

"Don't look so morose." Granqvist slapped him on the shoulder, though he looked just as anxious. "She's dangerous. She's right where she deserves to be. Any other fate would be too much of a risk to the Realm. To you."

"I know that." Realm's sake, no one knew that more than he did. "Just wish they'd turn on some lights in here."

"Small power generating station." Granqvist chuckled. "Little old to be afraid of the dark, aren't you, Westermark?"

"Westermark?" A creaky voice spoke from the nearest cell on his right, and Kresten came to an abrupt halt. Prisoners here, with the apparent exception of Zaella, knew better than to speak, especially to anyone from the Fleet. Speaking meant punishment, and more than that, it could mean hope—and there was no hope on 287X. "Lieutenant Kresten Westermark? The emperor's son?"

Granqvist gave an impatient nod toward the exit, accompanied by a slight roll of his eyes, but Kresten ground his boots into the floor and motioned for him to wait.

"Yes," he said, his apprehension building. "That's me. Do I know you?"

"No." The voice became stronger; a figure appeared in the shadows behind the force field, lithe and tall, his clothes hanging off boney shoulders. "But I heard of your wedding on Vilaria. Before I came here. I know about your wife. What she can do."

"And?" His response was curt, but what did this man expect? "What does that have to do with anything?"

"I thought you might be sympathetic. I thought you might understand."

"Mentioning my wife in this way is hardly the way to get my sympathy."

"You have to understand." The prisoner tucked a piece of ragged hair behind his ear. "I didn't do anything."

"Yeah." Granqvist folded his arms and gave a sigh of impatience. "I've never heard that one before. Quite the original defense."

Granqvist wasn't wrong in his sarcasm, and Kresten sighed as he turned to go. There wasn't anything to say, and the jumpship was waiting outside, fully fueled now.

"I could create fire," the prisoner called out.

Kresten froze, his hand on the keypad. "Create—" This man couldn't possibly think he'd show any pity for him. "Then it seems you're right where you should be. Let's get out of here, Granqvist."

"But it's not what you think," the man said, panicked. "They wouldn't listen to me. I could snap my fingers and create a spark, that's *all*. I could never even light a single candle. And they didn't listen. Accused me of—of so much. Forest fires and arson and murder. I never had a chance to defend myself."

"That's impossible." Granqvist took a step forward. "Surely you were telepathically questioned. You wouldn't be the first to hide your powers while in complete control of them."

"And your memories didn't lie," Kresten added. "Or you wouldn't be here."

"Telepaths do. Or can. Please, I meant no harm. You of all people must know we're not all dangerous and evil. You've got to help me."

"The law doesn't care how powerful you are," Granqvist replied. "Only that you have an innate gift—and you know that's forbidden."

"But it doesn't have to mean imprisonment. I researched it and learned there's a precedent. I can live with the suppression chip. I don't care if my power was gone forever; it was a curse, anyway. I just . . . I just can't live here."

"And what exactly do you want from me?" Kresten asked.

"Read my mind. Write a report, an accurate one. Beg someone, anyone. Just try to help me. That's all I'm asking."

Kresten rubbed his forehead. Realm's sake, a headache now? "I didn't decide your fate," he said, "and I have no say in it now." He glanced at the oxygen status monitor above the prisoner's cell. Normal, which meant the corridor was as well.

Which meant—well, hadn't he told Ryllis he wanted to *do* something? He hadn't expected to do it until they returned to Vilaria and he resumed his regular Shadow Force duties, but maybe there'd been a reason he and Granqvist had delivered Zaella to 287X when they did. Fate worked like that, didn't it?

"Westermark," Granqvist said under his breath. "Realm's sake, stop talking to him. He knows how badly we feel on his forsaken rock with all this misery around, and he's getting back at you the only way he knows how—by screwing with your mind even further."

"Maybe." Kresten put a hand on his shoulder and drew him away. "But you know this could have been me—oh, don't look at me like you don't know what I'm talking about. I know everyone in Shadow Force knows the story of the emperor's son who screwed up badly enough to be tortured by his own unit. By the Realm, it would have been you if you'd turned down an appointment to the Fleet. You're going to tell me that doesn't bother you on dark, lonely nights? That you aren't thinking about it now?"

Something flashed in Granqvist's eyes. Bitterness? Regret? It was impossible to tell with the grief floating around this place.

"You know I'm right," Kresten added.

Granqvist's shoulders stiffened. "I know he's playing you."

"Maybe. But if he is, it's not like I won't find out eventually." Kresten took a breath and turned back to the prisoner. "There's no medical facility here," he said. "And I can't move you from the asteroid to do it somewhere else. If you want me to question you, it'll hurt. Worse than the first time."

And that medic will probably be thrilled to see it.

"I don't care." The prisoner's lithe body straightened. "I just want the chance to clear myself."

"And I don't have any nanobiotes with me." Kresten slid his palms down the side of his pants, feeling the cylinder's absence. It had been a mistake leaving them on Cereth, but he hadn't thought he would have any need of them. "It will be several lunar cycles before I can return with some. But if you're willing to wait that long, I will do what I can."

"I see." The man's face fell. "Then I will wait as long as it takes."

Kresten nodded and turned toward the door once more.

"No need to return." Granqvist pulled a small vial from his pocket and shrugged at him before handing it over. "Some of us are always prepared."

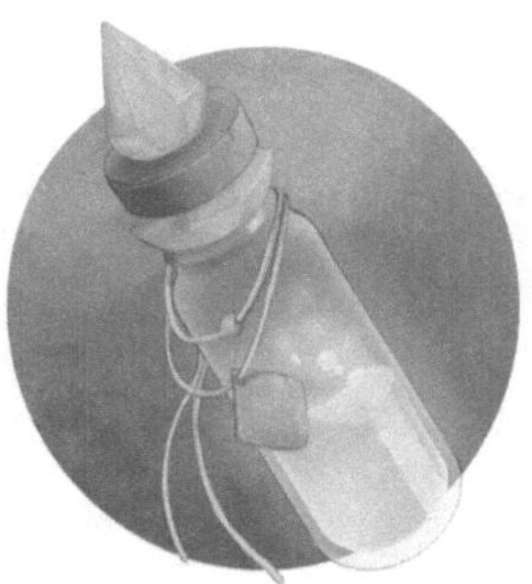

Kresten smiled as his hand closed over the tube. "Good thing, too."

A faint blue glow shimmered between his fingers, and for the first time in a long time, he didn't dread the process that was coming. If the man was guilty, he'd have only wasted a few hours on this rock—inconsequential in the grand scheme of things.

If not? Shadow Force needed to know. He would do this, he would file an *accurate* report, and then he would go back to Cereth or Vilaria or wherever else, and he would find out which telepath had lied.

And Ryllis would be waiting for him.

ACKNOWLEDGMENTS

Thanks, as always, to Meghan, Hope, and Cathy.

ABOUT THE AUTHOR

Anne Wheeler grew up with her nose in a book but earned two degrees in aviation before it occurred to her she was allowed to write her own. When not working, moving, or writing her next novel, she can be found planning her next escape to the desert—camera gear included. She currently lives in Georgia with her husband, son, and herd of cats.

For more information:
www.anne-wheeler.com